FIREBUG

DAVID BLAIR

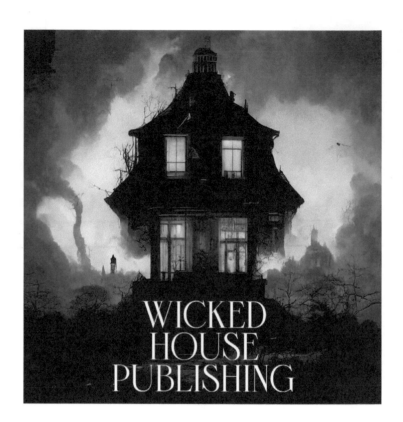

WICKED
HOUSE
PUBLISHING

Firebug
By David Blair

Wicked House Publishing

Cover design by Christian Bentulan
Interior Formatting by Joshua Marsella

CHAPTER ONE

I think it must've blown in with the wind. It was a particularly and peculiarly windy day when I first noticed strange things happening in my little town. I suppose it could have come here some other way: crawled out of the sewer maybe, or crash-landed from outer space, or summoned via séance by some stupid drunk assholes at a Christmas party. But I don't think so. I think it caught a ride on the wind. *That* wind on *that* day. Caught a ride from *some*where. I don't know where, but somewhere not *here*. Here as in Earth. Here as in reality.

Now, this coming from a guy who spent the better part of his first college semester high on LSD might cause you not to believe me. It's true the drugs and alcohol could have altered my brain somehow, made me *see* things that weren't there, *think* things that weren't true. But by the time *that* wind on *that* day blew, I was stone-cold sober and had been for two weeks. I didn't hallucinate the things that happened to my family and neighbors. Not even the worst imaginable trip could dream up the things I saw. Couldn't dream up *it*. And if it was a hallucination, it was a shared one because I wasn't the only person who saw it.

I'm wondering now, if through the infinitely mysterious intelligence of Mother Nature, that wind didn't somehow blow it straight to me.

I guess I could start with the night Chloe ran away, but I think I'll start before that.

I think I'll start with the car ride home from the university. My last.

It was the start of Thanksgiving Break and most everyone had left town, leaving the campus empty save for those whose families were locals. But unlike me, all the rest would be returning after the feasting holiday to all-nighters studying for finals, Christmas keggers, and general college-age merrymaking.

I was being ushered home by Mom and Dad for too much making merry before the appropriate season to do so. They'd heard (from a very reliable source) that since August I'd been attending nearly every class inebriated (which explained my worse-than-dismal grades), and they yanked me out of my freshman year faster than you can shoot tequila with a "Lick, drink, suck!"

Their actions weren't baseless or melodramatic in the least. The truth was I had become a high-functioning drunk in a matter of months, able to attend most classes under the guise of someone completely sober.

But, of course, there are always those who wish to ruin the party out of bitter jealousy and spite, and unfortunately my dorm mate's mother was good friends with my mother back home, and before long, word of my "habits" leaked back to Ferdinand and the jig was up. Isaac said he was "staging an intervention" and it was "for my own good," but really I think he was resentful of my reliable buyer and how said buyer kept me in vodka week after week. And I never shared.

"What are we? Pissed?"

It was the first time Dad had spoken since we loaded my stuff into the bed of his pickup and hit the road. Mom trailed us in my Corolla. I wondered why they didn't just let me drive my own car home, but then remembered: I was a prisoner now. They'd probably expected me to turn and flee if they'd let me behind the wheel, which I wouldn't have, but I could see why they'd think I might. Or maybe Dad just wanted some time alone so he could rip me a new asshole for pissing away a semester's worth of money he'd saved. That was probably more likely. And here it was, about to begin. Clench up, Daniel, this is gonna hurt.

"I'd hoped you'd feel ashamed," he continued. He took brief, sharp looks my way, but mostly kept his eyes on the road. Maybe it was because a snow flurry was suddenly cascading from the slate sky, which in Idaho could turn on a dime into a full-blown blizzard. Or maybe it was because he couldn't stand to look at me, his failure of a son, for any length of time longer than a blink.

"Maybe a little bit of both, son?"

I stared out the window with my forehead against the cold glass, my breath fogging a circle on it. The highway we traveled was flanked with pine trees, and they sped past in a blur of green. He was right, I did feel both. But honestly, in that moment I mostly just really wanted to beat the shit out of Isaac. What a little bitch.

"You have every right to be angry with your mom and me, Daniel. You do. But you know something? We have *more* of a right to be angry with *you*. Which we are. You bet your ass we are. Furious. But even more than that?"

Uh oh, here it comes, the dreaded D-word.

"We're disappointed in you, Daniel."

Yup. There it is.

"Again."

Whoa, wasn't expecting that. *Again.* I lifted my head off the glass and finally looked at my father. He was watching the road with a furrowed brow. The way he'd said *Again* was like he was exhausted by it, like it physically wore him out to say it. Or I wore him out for having to say it.

This welled within me a horrible self-pitying darkness, and I briefly contemplated lifting the door latch and throwing myself out onto the highway. Instead, I said, "Well sorry, Dad, I'm just a big failure, huh! Just a huge waste of flesh. Sorry you raised such a disappointment!"

"Knock it off," he said, utterly unaffected by my *I'm the victim* act. He flipped on the wipers as the flurry increased, becoming a full-fledged snowfall. I glared at him, hating him for knowing my tricks and weapons and how to instantly disarm me. I returned my forehead to the window, with some dramatic force so he'd know my anger. A little too dramatic, actually. I winced.

Through the corner of my eye, I could see Dad's head making those quick turns, his eyes giving those brief looks, and I heard him draw breath like he was about to speak. Maybe to start really yelling, giving one of his classic lectures that have always made me want to gouge my eardrums with forks and rip all my hair out. Maybe apologize for bringing up the past unfoundedly, a past he was in part responsible for, and while, yes, I did nearly burn the house down on more than one occasion (and succeeded in torching someone else's), it had nothing to do with my current set of habits.

In the end, he returned his full attention to the road and said nothing. He reached forward and turned on the radio. The Beach Boys were on, calling to "Hoist up the John B.'s sail..." and I thought it an oddly fitting song to be playing right now. This wasn't necessarily the worst trip I'd ever been on, 'cause trust me, I'd been on some doozies.

But it was damn close.

I grew up in the unassuming and forgettable town of Ferdinand in the equally unassuming and forgettable state of Idaho. It was the kind of small country town where nothing— and I mean *nothing*—ever happens. Not even the popular meth problems that are now a part of small-town existence were issues in Ferdinand. We had zero drama in my little town, save for the occasional bar fight, the expected adolescent delinquency, and maybe the fleeting rumor of someone's infidelity.

Timber harvesting, farming, and agriculture were the big economies, so if you didn't own a farm, weren't related to someone who owned a farm, didn't specialize in the maintenance of farming equipment, or operate a farm-to-market, there was only one question to ask yourself: What in the hell am I doing here? With a dwindling population of only 1,500, Ferdinand barely existed at all.

When we finally pulled into town, it looked, predictably, just the same as when I'd left. Of course, I'd only been gone for three months, and even in a more progressive community, not a lot changes in three months. The only differences were that where before the lawns had been green and host to those peaceful sprinklers that always remind me of harps, there was now a blanket of ever-thickening white, and the marquee on the Blue Fox Theater had changed from the most recent Marvel film to a double feature of *It's a Wonderful Life* and *Scrooged* with Bill Murray.

Not even Thanksgiving yet, I thought. *But I'm not surprised.*

My kid siblings were both excited to have me home for Thanksgiving, but only Soren, my fourteen-year-old brother knew I'd be staying well past that. Lilly, who'd just turned eight, greeted me at the door with the tightest hug I think I'd ever felt, with our German shepherd Chloe nosing her way into my crotch welcoming me home, the lost member of the pack. Soren greeted me with a shit-eating grin.

"What's up, alkie?"

"I'd kick in your teeth if I thought it wouldn't improve your face."

Soren flipped me his middle finger when Mom's back was turned.

We all took turns ladling soup from a big pot of Progresso Mom had heated up. Brown chunks of beef splashed into my bowl and left drops of thick broth on the ceramic glass stovetop which I unabashedly left behind.

"There's garlic bread in the oven," said Mom, gesturing to me to take it out. I ignored her and sat down at the dinner table next to Soren. Mom's tongue poked the inside of her cheek, something she often did when aggravated, and with a sigh she reached for an oven mitt. Rather than poke an angry bear, she changed the subject.

"Soren, how was your math test?"

Soren slurped on his spoon. "It sucked."

"Because math sucks," I opined. "If I hadn't cheated my way through, I never would have graduated high school."

Mom tossed the bag of garlic bread down in front of me with her mitted hand. It shook my silverware. "You're such a great influence on your siblings, Dan. Ignore your brother, Soren, math can be fun, and it's arguably the most important subject in school. It's really the universal language."

"Arguably," I said with clear recalcitrance. Mom and I were fixing to go to war.

"I thought love was the universal language," said Dad, tearing open the steamy bag of bread.

"What does 'universal language' mean?" asked Lilly, mindlessly stirring her beef and veggies as if she were mixing a witch's brew.

Mom took a seat at the table and placed a rectangle of paper towel on her knee. "It means a language that everyone in the world can use to communicate without using words. Please eat your soup, baby, it doesn't need to be stirred."

"What do you wanna be when you grow up, Soren?" I asked, ripping off a piece of garlic bread.

Soren shrugged. "I dunno. President?"

"President! Perfect! You don't need to know math to be President! You don't need to know shit to be President, just look at Trump!"

"That's enough, Dan," said Dad.

"Oh, sorry, I know you voted for him."

Dad cracked a smile, but it was without mirth. "I didn't, but even if I had, it'd be none of your business."

"None of my business? You're my father, you raised me

7

with your particular belief systems and values, how are your politics none of my business?" Fixing to go to war with Dad. His eyes on me were unwavering and I could practically see his blood pressure rising.

"I want to be a horse trainer when I grow up," Lilly offered.

"Nobody asked you," said Soren.

"Soren," Mom scolded.

Dad's eyes were still fixed on me. "Okay," he started, his tone still amiable enough to consider this a levelheaded conversation. "You clearly have something you want to say. Speak your mind, Daniel. Let's hear it."

"You know exactly what's on my mind, Dad. This whole situation is bullshit."

Dad set his spoon down, and with it, his amiable tone. "What specifically about the situation is bullshit, Daniel? I'd really like to get your take on it because what I find bullshit is your illegal drinking, your shitty grades, wasting mine and your mother's money so you can screw off when you should be taking your education seriously, and this attitude you have like you're somehow entitled to do whatever the hell you want. So tell me, son, what's bullshit, huh?" Dad's face had gone red and Mom's displayed scorn for his frequent cursing in front of the children. He didn't notice.

I did what I always do after a verbal wallop: deflected with a look away, a laugh through my teeth and a shake of the head. "You totally uprooted me and brought me back home. Do you know how humiliating that is?"

Dad slurped his soup. "You'll get no sympathy from me."

"Wow, I'm shocked," I said.

"We're trying to help, Daniel," said Mom gently. "We're not the enemy here."

"You *should* be humiliated," Dad continued. "A nineteen-year-old with as much potential as you have does not belong living at home with Mom and Dad because he squandered his future away."

"What does *squander* mean?" asked Lilly.

Not missing a beat, Dad said, "It means to foolishly waste something very important, sweetheart."

A hundred tiny detonations set off in my chest, the rubble and smoke and fire rising up my throat, choking my lungs. I could feel the lightning-bright stabs of fury threatening to short-circuit my brain.

I fixed Dad with raised eyebrows and spoke in the most condescending tone I could muster. "Are you done? 'Cause if this is going to go on, I'm liable to say some things you don't wanna hear, so I suggest we just eat our soup."

Dad dropped his spoon in his bowl and released a genuine guffaw. Yes—a guffaw. My blood boiled.

"Did you just threaten me, son?" Dad asked.

The sudden look in his eyes made my testicles retreat into my body. If I hadn't been skating on thin ice before, I certainly was now and I expected at any moment for Mom to tell me so.

"You're skating on thin ice here, Dan," she said. Yep, right on cue.

Soren snickered. "This is awesome."

Leave. Just leave the table. Cut your losses and get out of here. But my perplexing need to come out on top of this argument (which was never going to happen) far outweighed my brain's insistence to take the high road. I was already in too deep. Story of my life.

9

"I just think it's funny how…" I made my fingers into air quotes— "parental you're being right now. That's all."

Dad turned to Mom, a fiery gleam in his eye. "Oh, he'd rather us not give a shit, let him ruin his life."

"Stop DOING THAT, talk to ME!" I pounded both fists on the table, which was enough to rattle the cutlery and bounce Dad's soup bowl off the edge and into his lap. Chair legs squealed against the hardwood floor as he backed away, cursing at the hot liquid spilled on his crotch. He stood, his bowl clanking to the floor, and when his eyes met mine, I knew I was defeated.

"You should excuse yourself," he said, a smoking volcano overdue for an eruption. "Right now."

Soup dripped off his jeans. For once, Soren was stunned into silence. Lilly just stared at me, and Mom stared at Dad.

I got up from the table with just enough of an attitude to convey my lack of apology and walked out of the kitchen like I'd won despite the overwhelming evidence against it.

It took a few days for our relationship to recover. We passed each other in the house like strangers in a subway. It was clear the tension was affecting the rest of the family, but we're both stubborn men and neither of us cared to make the first move toward reconciliation, no matter how thickly our uncomfortable silences teargassed our home.

Three days after Dad's soup met his lap, he finally asked me to help him dig the Christmas lights out of the garage. "Asked" is a funny way of putting it because I didn't really have a choice. So, we found the boxes marked "X-Mas Lights

—house (outside), tree, and house (inside)" and began sorting and untangling. Through the course of the project, we said our apologies and quickly moved on. Dad was never one to linger on feelings, and honestly, if we'd gone any deeper I knew my anger would unfurl its wings again and take to the sky, a dragon bent on scorching the planet. Bygones were bygones.

For all intents and purposes, I was under house arrest (*Again*). Mom worked as an accountant for a handful of local farmers and could do most of her job from home, so I was under constant surveillance. I was allowed to run errands and do little jobs around the house, so it wasn't like I wasn't kept busy.

Mom humiliatingly signed me up for Alcoholics Anonymous, which met bi-weekly at the Shriner's Lodge, and so on Tuesdays and Thursdays I shamefully drove my "addicted" ass through town to sit with a bunch of recovering drunks and talk about Jesus. For a town of only fifteen hundred I was surprised at the number of attendants. Apparently, the humdrum existence of living in Ferdinand had driven more than a few men and women to the bottle. *Not* surprising when I think about it.

It came to my attention that Isaac had evidently not told his mother about my acid bender (or my affinity for marijuana, for that matter) as all anyone seemed to mention when asking why I'd come back home was a problem with alcohol. Yes, I liked to get drunk, *loved* it in fact, but I never turned down a laced Altoid and the opportunity to trip my balls off either. I liked all the poisons equally and gave them all equal chances to show me a good time. But if all I was going to get busted for was drinking, I'd take it.

My punishment would have undoubtedly been more severe had my folks learned I'd been experimenting with hallucinogens. I'd probably get trucked off to rehab, maybe even the mental institution in Boise. I could definitely kiss any chance of going back to the university goodbye.

Mom and Dad said that if I showed them I could act responsibly and stay dry, they might consider funding another semester. But that was a long way off. A very long way off. They gave me the feeling I might be in my thirties before they'd put so much as a dime toward my continued education.

Mom and Dad, not heavy drinkers to begin with, had either hidden or emptied what few bottles of booze they did have. Usually, a bottle of whiskey or Scotch could be found in the pantry, or maybe a fifth of Absolut in the freezer, but now any and all things containing alcohol (including the Nyquil) were nowhere to be found. I know this because after that first week I went looking. And I should have known they'd prepared the house for my homecoming, doing away with all the self-destructive devices because they'd had to do it before. Only that time, it wasn't liquor they'd had to get rid of.

One morning after my shower, I stood naked in front of the bathroom mirror and for the first time noticed how my body had changed since I'd gone to college. *Sunken* was the word that came to mind, though I could have picked *sickly, atrocious,* or *what-little-sex-appeal-there-was-in-high-school-is-now-gone*. My usually bright blue eyes were now dull and nestled deep within purple hollows. My cheeks stuck out. I could see my ribs.

How in the hell did I not notice this before? I thought.

Because you were inside the tornado, a voice said inside my head. *Now you're out and can see the damage.*

I studied my face. Most things were the same as before. My stubble of beard had always been patchy, but Dad assured me that one day it would fill in. My nose was big, perhaps a touch too big for my face, but my ex-girlfriend, Beth, used to say how she thought it was sexy, and how it had been one of the things that had attracted her to me in the first place. Plus, she'd always heard that the size of a guy's nose is in direct proportion to the size of his you-know-what, so the bigger the nose, the bigger the you-know-what. She hadn't been disappointed.

But my eyes and my suddenly sharpened cheeks. Those were new.

I sighed and got dressed. The odyssey of putting the Christmas lights on the house was beginning today, and my participation was expected. It was an all-hands-on-deck sort of thing, and even with five of us helping, the way Dad liked the house to look could take days. I'm sure a lot of American dads are compared to Clark Griswold from *National Lampoon's Christmas Vacation* and my dad is no exception. If you can't see our house from Mars, we failed.

The day the Christmas lights project started, there were six inches of snow on the ground. Frequent trips indoors had to be made for our fingers and toes to thaw out. The day the project was completed, not a single white patch remained anywhere. During the course of a single night, a Chinook wind had blown through the Camas Prairie and eaten all the snow. It was that night wind which continued into the day that was the bringer of the something I keep talking about. The *it*, the *thing*, the *monster*. While we festooned the last

13

remaining front yard bushes with multi-colored lights, some-thing was coming to town, and it sure as hell wasn't Santa Claus. *Alien* is another word I can think of to describe it, though not in the *It Came from Outer Space* sense (though it could have).

No other word fits. Except for maybe *hungry*.

Mom had gone inside with Lilly to start dinner. It was the three men left to finish, and the dog. Our first family pet, a cocker spaniel named Yummy was the worst dog on the planet. You could not trust Yummy to be alone and un-kenneled, to be in the kitchen, or to be in the front yard unleashed. That little bastard would bolt in a heartbeat and be halfway down the block before you even knew he'd flown the coup. He got run over by a 4-Runner when he was only two. Chloe, on the other hand, was the opposite. She was well behaved and as obedient a dog as you could hope for. Before that night, she'd only run away once before. It was around the Fourth of July and Soren and I were blowing off firecrackers in the backyard. The ear-splitting pops were too much for her nerves to bear and we watched as she literally climbed the chain link fence to escape. It was an incredible thing to witness, even though I felt bad for having driven her to such a desperately panicked stunt. We found her later, a few blocks away, hiding in the culvert that runs under Maple Street. She was sitting in ankle-deep creek water looking like a child orphaned in a war-torn city.

But right then she was sitting calmly on the front lawn, watching her alpha and two betas string lights and tie down the holiday rooftop inflatables. Soren and I wove the lights in and around the pine bush while Dad climbed the ladder with a giant blow-up snowman. The Chinook wind continued to blow, ruffling our hair and jackets.

"Dad, be careful," I said, throwing a glance over my shoulder at him. He reached the rooftop and blithely scaled it with the snowman in his grip, his feet crunching on the shingles.

"Your old man's a pro, Danny boy."

Chloe suddenly rose to her feet as if something had startled her. I thought at first she'd just spotted Dad on the roof, her curiosity piqued. This was not a normal place for her master to be, after all, and she looked a touch concerned, her ears spiked. But her sharp nose led her in a tight circle, her black nostrils quivering rapidly as she sniffed the breeze. I followed her gaze up into the sky, searching for whatever had grabbed her attention, expecting to see a flock of birds or maybe a dancing grocery sack caught in the wind. There was nothing but clear sky. Then she started to whine. And then growl. This finally got Soren's attention and like me, he trained his eyes on the sky.

"What is it, girl?"

When her growl erupted into a snarling machine-gun bark, I think we all flinched. Dad leaned over the edge of the rooftop for a look.

"What's got her going?"

She looked as if she'd just treed a defenseless kitty cat and was *yap-yap-yapping* at the little thing hiding in the branches. But there was no cat and no tree. She was simply barking like mad at the sky.

"Soren, take her inside, would ya?" said Dad, turning back to his inflatable snowman. "She'll have every dog in the neighborhood goin'."

But I could already hear the sounds of the local canines rising up. I knew of a few neighbors with dogs—one a golden retriever just two houses down from ours, the other a miniature pinscher on the other side of the block—and could hear their distinguishable barks overlapping Chloe's. Soren grabbed her by the collar, and she whirled around, struggling against his grip.

"Jesus, what's the matter, girl?" he said, pulling her back toward the front door. It was taking all his strength to control her. She was no chihuahua, after all. Beneath her black and rust-colored coat I could see her muscles tighten as she resisted Soren hauling her backwards. I searched the sky again, but vainly.

Who knows what sets dogs off sometimes? Their senses are far more refined than any human's, and I think sometimes they have a few extra, too. They know before an earthquake strikes, are rumored to see ghosts, and some have even been reported to know if someone has cancer just by the smell, for Christ's sake. But they also bark at mailboxes. And ours is afraid of the vacuum cleaner. So right then, I thought maybe she'd seen a cloud she didn't like or caught a whiff of pussycat from down the road.

After muttering a few expletives under his breath, Soren finally disappeared behind the front door with Chloe, the dog still losing her mind. I could still hear her barking even with the door closed. But above that, I heard not just the golden and the pinscher, but countless other dogs suddenly take up the call. It was like every dog in Ferdinand had heard Chloe's distress and was responding in kind. The air was suddenly cluttered with barking.

"Daniel," came my father's voice from the rooftop. "Get up here. Come look at this."

By the bewildered tone of Dad's voice, I knew he wasn't calling me up to inspect the snowman.

I climbed the ladder, the warm wind tossing about the loose flaps of my opened jacket, and I couldn't help but feel a nostalgic tug at my heart for those times when it was just Mom, Dad, and me, before Soren and Lilly were born. Dad would often use that same tone, excited to show his baby boy something magical for the first time like a full moon or a praying mantis, wanting to see the wonderment brighten his boy's face. It had still happened every now and again even after the other two came along, but it stopped after I'd taken a shine to open flame. And I certainly didn't expect that it would return after screwing up my first college semester. But I heard it then, calling conspiratorially for me to join him on the rooftop.

When I crested the eaves, I found him with his back turned, staring at something far off behind our house. In the dying, slanted light of late afternoon, the way he stood sure-footed upon a steeply angled surface brought to mind an image of something anciently heroic, like a traveler discovering new lands or a king surveying his kingdom. I crunched my way across the shingles to take up beside him and glanced at his face. I think for the first time in my nineteen years, it occurred to me then that my dad might be handsome. His nose was a little big, like mine, and he had a slight paunch, but his shoulders were broad and square (he'd played football in high school and always said that's where he got his "rockin' bod") and he still had a full head of black hair and a kind face. I think the way the waning light hit him might have lit up his blue eyes a little, maybe erased a few wrinkles here and there, causing him to look not like Dad, but like someone valiant.

Behind our backyard was a small field that once held two horses but was now just an empty pasture with a few apple trees. Beyond that was the Raddock Addition, a slightly higher-end neighborhood that was known around town as "Snob Knob." It wasn't rich by the world's standards but to the common Ferdinandian it was. From our rooftop vantage point, we could see into the backyards of three Raddock Addition homes, and it was into these backyards my father's bright, sunlit eyes kept darting. He pointed to them, but I knew what had captured his interest before he even spoke.

"Look. The dogs."

In those backyards, dogs of various breeds, both large and small, were behaving exactly as Chloe had: snouts in the air, baying at some unseen menace. I spun around to see if I had a view into the golden's backyard and could plainly see him, standing almost dead center, snarling and barking at the wind as if it were a burglar attempting a break-in.

"What's going on?" I asked, but I knew Dad's guess was as good as mine.

The chorus of barking dogs seemed to grow as we stood there on the roof, yips and yaps and howls carried by the wind from all four corners of town. From across the county. Every dog in Idaho it seemed.

"Beats the shit outta me," Dad replied.

I didn't know it then, but I'm pretty sure I know it now.

It had just arrived.

CHAPTER TWO

By dinnertime, the Chinook wind had blown itself out and left behind a cold, eerie stillness. The forecasters said that creeping just behind the winds was a dark mass of clouds, and a gathering snowstorm was expected to drop at least a foot of the white stuff on the Camas Prairie. By bedtime, it had begun. Idaho weather: turning on a dime.

I watched through my bedroom window as the snow fell in colossal flakes past the glow of the tall streetlight on the corner. It fell fast, as if the storm had gone into overdrive and just couldn't wait to bury us. There was an oddly beautiful tranquility about it though, and I thought the only thing that could make this moment perfect was if I'd had a Vodka Collins in my hand. Or a Vodka Red Bull. Or even a good ol' fashioned Keystone. If I'd had a joint to go with it, that'd be even better.

At my first AA meeting, they'd said if I ever had the urge to drink I should call my sponsor. At present time, my sponsor was my mother and I didn't really feel like waking her up. Besides, I wasn't an addict. I wasn't dependent upon alcohol to get me through the day like most of my fellow Anons. I just really liked to party. So what? That didn't make me an addict. I just thought that a drink, preferably something strong to warm the insides on this winter's night, would take this moment to the next level. Watching the snow falling is great, and at night when the streetlights light it up so you can see it dropping is downright gorgeous. But if I were to have a nice stiff cocktail to go along with it? Sublime.

That night I dreamt I was a fireman. Not the sort that puts out fires, but rather the sort that starts them, like they do in Bradbury's *Fahrenheit 451*. I had a flamethrower in my hands and was igniting the university commons, watching dozens of frightened and confused students flee with schoolbooks and backpacks in hand, running for their lives. I couldn't understand it—didn't they know this was my job? Why all the terror? I think Mom and Dad were in there somewhere, too. I woke up in a cold sweat at 3:38 a.m. and the snow was still coming down.

The night Chloe ran away, the part I've been meaning to get to since I started this story, was the night of Lilly's Christmas pageant. It was also the night I saw *it* for the first time, and the start of the unraveling of the universe. I always think of a cat whose claw has snagged the loose end of a ball of yarn and keeps pulling and pulling until the ball isn't a ball anymore, just a puddled mess of string, undone and disarrayed. That's how I felt. That's what became of my grip on the known universe. That's the night I discovered that some things *exist*, whether you like it or not. Whether you *believe* it or not. Those things that you've only ever seen in movies or on TV, or read about in books, or maybe just thought about in your wild and crazy imagination...

Let's just say the idea of Santa Claus being real, or

leprechauns or the devil suddenly didn't seem so absurd after that night.

It was December 14th, a Friday. Lilly's pageant was at six, so we'd planned on an early dinner that night. Mom was in the kitchen, boiling water for pasta and talking on the phone. I think we lived in the only part of the country where most everyone still had a landline. In the boonies, cell reception isn't the greatest, so it's necessary. I was coming out of my bedroom and heading down the hallway with the intention of taking Chloe for a quick walk before dinner. I stopped just short of where the hall leads into the kitchen when I heard Mom mention my name to whomever she was chatting with. Her voice was low, as if the topic of conversation was private and not meant to be overheard. I peeked around the corner and saw Mom at the stovetop with the phone propped between her shoulder and her cheek, the spiral cord stretched so far the curl was nearly gone from it. She was adding the pasta and didn't see me. I decided I'd like to eavesdrop and so ducked back behind the corner.

"We have no idea. For as long as it takes, I suppose," she said.

A pause as whoever it was spoke.

"Well, I appreciate the encouragement."

Pause. A longer one this time.

"He's a good kid, really he is. He's just made some bad choices."

I guess that's true, but I hate that old clichéd axiom. It always sounds like a cop out or an excuse. Actually, I am a good kid who has taken his choices (neither good nor bad) a little too far. Society doesn't always like that. But Mom was defending me, and for that, I couldn't roll my eyes.

Pause. The person on the other end must not have agreed with her because then she said something that made me really love her.

"Well, you don't know him like I do."

She'd been talking to Sharon Fitzmaurice from down the block and had volunteered me to shovel the Fitzmaurice's driveway while they were away on Christmas vacation. Apparently, Mom had spoken to several people from the neighborhood and volunteered me to do the same for them as well. Some were reluctant, given my history, and afraid I might relapse and burn their homes to the ground. But some had not only agreed, they'd insisted they pay me. Mom tactfully put the kibosh on that, telling them that it would be done simply because it's the neighborly thing to do, and we were one of three families on the block not leaving town for the holidays. It only made sense. In actuality, she didn't particularly want me having my own money yet as she feared I might persuade someone of legal drinking age to buy me booze with it. So, my list of chores got longer and longer until I accused Mom and Dad of using me for slave labor. They'd looked at each other and smiled, and then agreed. Jerks.

We arrived at Ferdinand Elementary a full hour before the pageant was scheduled to begin because Lilly had to get into costume, and Mom was helping run the refreshments table and had to set up. Dad and I found front row seats and set our coats and scarves across five to save them, then wandered the arcade looking into the trophy cases along the walls. Soren and his odd little emo friend Erik sat outside on the benches, gossiping and looking cool.

Dad found the old football photo, circa '79, and waved me over so I could see what a strapping lad he'd been. I'd already seen it about six million times but obliged with a smile (after rolling my eyes first, of course). Through the glass, we stared at the framed washed-out color photo, and Dad pointed out some of his buddies on the team. I stared at the 1979-version of my father and thought that could have been me standing there in shoulder pads with sweat-slicked hair. We were nearly carbon copies, but only in the physical sense. I never played football in high school, or any sport for that matter, and didn't share any of my father's interests, then or now.

In high school I was a band geek and hung out with the perverted artsy kids. In an arena like high school, our social circles never would have interacted, except for the times when jocks shove geeks into lockers. There's a poem by some guy named Kipling that comes to mind, one I remember hearing in English Lit 101 (which is saying something because I was usually three sheets to the wind in English Lit), and there's a part that goes, "East is East, and West is West, and never the twain shall meet." That's my father and me. If we'd known each other in high school, we'd never have been friends. We just wouldn't have anything in common. He was now an agricultural biologist; a profession I'd always found terribly boring and had often wondered what possessed him to go into such a field. I liked music and hoped to one day make a career out of it, which vexed my father. To him music was, at best, just a hobby. At worst, a distraction from whatever else I could be doing to eventually make a living.

But looks-wise, if the 1979 version of Dad had been standing beside me right then, you wouldn't have been able to tell us apart. It always tripped me out to see old pictures of Dad. Genetics are astounding.

Out of the blue, Dad said, "I wanna say sorry for the other day. In the truck bringing you home. That was wrong of me to bring that up."

It caught me off guard and at first, I didn't even know what he was talking about.

Then I remembered. The *Again*.

"You don't have to say anything, I just want to apologize for that. Look'ee here! That's Dennis Weaver!" A laugh. "He was a character!"

That's all I would get from him, and honestly, it was more than I expected. He didn't like bringing up that point in time, almost as much as he didn't like apologizing. But he'd done both just now, and I was speechless. I guess I'd call it a Christmas miracle.

In the elementary school auditorium, the curtain went up precisely at six. The place was packed, and the general collage of pre-show audience noise (chit-chat, ruffling programs, squeaky chairs) died almost at once. Revealed behind the red velvet curtain were three tiered rows of second and third graders standing on risers that stretched across the stage. They opened the show with a rousing, though mostly off-key rendition of "Do You Hear What I Hear." Lilly stood on the middle riser, stage right, and found us in the audience immediately, her face lighting up with a huge smile. She, along with several other girls were dressed as cowgirls. A few boys were dressed as cowboys, and a few others donned felt ears and had their faces painted to look like horses.

For the next number, a small pine tree was wheeled out and all the cowgirls scampered off-stage only to return several seconds later with their props. The canned music kicked in and all at once the cowgirls were decorating the tree with colored balls and strings of popcorn and tinsel while singing "We Need a Little Christmas." Lilly seemed to disregard her responsibility to sing, so wrapped up was she in the decorating part. Good thing she had a few enthusiastic divas to fill the gap, and those little girls drowned out most everyone else anyway.

Beside me, Soren and Emo Erik kept whispering and sniggering, so I reached over and smacked Soren upside the head. He scowled and punched me hard in the thigh. Erik just kept sniggering. I know it sounds awful, but I really wanted to smack Erik too based solely on his appearance. His hair was cut in this strange faux-hawk/mullet thing that's popular with the kids these days, and he was squeezed into a low-riding pair of skinny jeans that had to be crushing whatever balls he had. God, I hate skinny jeans. No male should ever wear skinny jeans. And he wore those trendy, thick-framed hipster glasses that are supposed to be ironically cool, but just made him look like a douche. Mom wore a pair of those too, but hers were a little tamer and made her look, quite honestly, adorable. On Emo Erik, they screamed, *"I'm trying really hard to look like what's cool now."* But I guess at fourteen, that's what everybody does. I didn't care. I still wanted to smack that little brat.

Mom leaned forward in her chair and met us with raised eyebrows, giving that look that is universally understood by misbehaving children everywhere: *"Knock it off or so help me..."* Soren responded with another universally understood expression, the one that says, *"Don't look at me, he started it."* Someone behind us cleared their throat, the understood theater expression for *"Quit fucking around up there, you're ruining the show."*

"We Need a Little Christmas" ended, and the cowgirls wheeled the newly decorated tree off stage to roaring applause and dozens of "Aws" and "Ohs" and "Isn't that darling?" Next the cowboys and horses took center stage and sang an unfamiliar song, presumably written by the pageant director, who suddenly sprang from the left wing and plopped herself down in front of a piano. No canned music for *her* masterpiece. Something about "...Christmas on the range," and "Even cowboys get a visit from ol' St. Nick," and some other shit. I'm sure all the actual cowboys in the audience got a kick out of that one, which, judging from the number of black Stetson hats I'd seen, constituted about three-quarters of it. That little number led into an awkward square dance (or was it an awkward *line* dance?) between the cowboys, cowgirls, and horses. This got the audience clapping to the beat, and I wouldn't have been surprised to see a handful of those fervent spectators suddenly on their feet and square dancing in the aisles.

The second and third graders were granted a small reprieve as the red velvet curtain closed and a quartet of fifth graders (two girls, two boys) took center stage and sang a Christmas medley of "Silver Bells" and "White Christmas." They were good, all harmonized and everything, but quite frankly, bored me. I wanted those unpredictable, unpolished tiny tots back. Plus, I really loved seeing my baby sister up there, all glowy and proud to be on stage, performing in front of everyone.

The medley ended, the fifth graders bowed and exited, and the velvet curtain was drawn once again. The tiny Christmas tree had been wheeled back on stage, but someone in the meantime had strung it with lights, and it now glowed blue and white. The canned music started and all at once a small girl was belting out the first lyrics of "Have Yourself a Merry Little Christmas." This was to be the finale of the show, and almost every student had been assigned one line of the song to sing solo. Lilly had "…From now on our troubles will be out of sight." Next, a little redhead sang, "Have yourself a merry little Christmas…" and after her, it was a boy's turn. Perhaps it was a cruel confluence of elements created merely by chance, or perhaps the director was a sadistic heartless bitch. Or perhaps I'm over-thinking it entirely and it all comes down to the maddening immaturity of fourteen-year-olds.

The boy had the tiniest lisp, and was dressed in a bright red vest, and sang his solo with enough vim and vigor to give those divas in his class a run for their money. "…Make the Yuletide gaaay…" he sang.

The joke was too irresistible for Soren and Emo Erik and the two deflated their lungs with a *pffff* through teeth and lips, hunching down in their seats and leaning into each other.

I'd had it.

I leaned into them and practically spat the words out. "Grow up, you idiots."

Soren, used to his older brother's insults, ignored me and continued giggling into his fist. Erik stifled his laughter long enough to give me a look that said I was the most pathetic, insubstantial *nobody* he'd ever been confronted by.

"What do you know, *firebug*?"

My response was cocked and ready. *"Eat my nuts, Jared Leto"* was on the tip of my tongue. But so caught off guard was I to hear that old word, that old nickname, that the rebuke stayed in my mouth. Firebug. I'd wondered earlier if

Sharon Fitzmaurice hadn't brought up that same topic in the phone conversation with Mom, maybe even using the same word. My reputation in this little town was neither gone nor forgotten, it seemed. It remained, like the odor of last night's dinner. Or a ghost haunting an old house. Or maybe it had died, but my disgraced return had pulled it from its grave.

Firebug.

Suddenly I was no longer in the elementary school auditorium, but a boy of twelve hovering over a bathroom wastebasket on fire. I'd dropped the flaming Kleenex into it just to see what would happen. And it had been incredible.

When I didn't respond Erik gave another one of those *pffff's*, shook his head, and sat back in his seat. I must have looked stupid, staring at him expressionless and with no comeback. A lame fourteen-year-old had completely thrown me, and that realization suddenly made me feel even more impotent. I sat back in my chair and watched the remainder of "Have Yourself a Merry Little Christmas." At the end, all the children bowed to applause and whistles and cheers. A few people in the audience gave a standing ovation. The red velvet curtain fell and the house lights came on.

But that word was echoing in my ears, and I hardly noticed any of it.

We stayed for punch and cookies and fudge and milled around with the other families. Mom cheerfully took people's money at the refreshments table while another parent handed out the treats, and Dad and I stood off to the side. Dad struck up a conversation with another father, and I was left to munch on my chocolate chip cookies and stand awkward and alone like the dorky kid on the playground without any friends.

I did see Isaac (the rat!) in the crowd, and for half a second considered going over and giving him a piece of my mind. He was clear across the auditorium and in the company of his family, and truth be told, the anger I'd felt toward him had lost its strength, so I stayed put. He didn't see me, and if he did, he pretended not to. I finished off my last cookie and let it go. What was done was done.

I saw a few other peers of mine in the crowd as well, and in particular, a girl I used to like named Rebecca Bailey. She saw me and waved. I waved back. We never dated (I'd hooked up with Beth by the time we finally noticed one another), but I'd jerked off to her many a night and considered dumping Beth several times with the hope of my fantasies one day coming true. We'd flirted in Government class almost every day, but nothing ever came of it. Seeing her right then I thought I might go over and rekindle whatever it was we'd had (which was little more than playful banter and good-natured ribbing), but she turned and headed out of the building with some other guy. Looked like some college hipster boyfriend. C'est la vie. And was that a "baby bump"? Ok, maybe more serious than a boyfriend. Seeing her, though, made me think I'd probably revisit some of those fantasies later tonight, baby bump or no.

By eight, we were headed out the auditorium doors and into a night speckled with falling snow. A few fresh inches had already accrued and at the rate it was falling, we'd probably see another four by morning. We grabbed Soren, who'd engaged in a snowball fight with Erik and a few other boys in the elementary school parking lot. I scooped up a big handful of snow and could not resist the urge. As hard as I could, I threw and scored a direct hit in Erik's face. To my delight, his hipster glasses flew right off and the other boys laughed at him. Take that, shithead.

On the ride home Lilly was a veritable chatterbox. The thrill of performing had given her the biggest buzz, and she couldn't stop talking about the audience and the applause, couldn't quit begging for validation with "Are you sure I did okay?" and "Did I sound as good as Stephanie Fredrickson?" and "Wasn't my dancing wonderful?"

Everyone in the car fed her exactly what she needed to hear except for me because I'd gone back in time. I was twelve again and wondering what would happen if I touched a lit match to the plastic-covered wedding dress hanging in Mom's closet. I fortunately never got to see because a seven-year-old Soren had come bounding down the hall and surely would have told on me if he'd seen what I'd been up to.

Firebug.

I started to recall the first time I'd heard that word but didn't get too far down Memory Lane before our radiant beacon of a house came into view. We weren't the only ones on the block who'd decorated, but it was a safe bet that our electric bill would be the highest next month. Dad hit the button on the garage door opener as we turned onto our snow-packed driveway.

In the warm months, we'd leave Chloe in the backyard whenever we left the house. During the winter, we made a little nest out of old blankets and left her in the garage, safe from the cold wind and weather. We'd leave the door leading from the backyard into the garage opened, however, so she could go outside to relieve herself if she needed. When we'd come home during those cold months, we'd usually find her sitting in the middle of her nest, tail wagging double-time, anxious for us to pull into the garage so she could greet us.

As the garage door slowly lifted, her nest of old blankets was empty.

My first thought was that something was wrong. I really had no reason to think that other than she hadn't really been herself since *that* wind on *that* day, but suddenly I could feel the chest-gripping fist of alarm as my mind began creating irrational scenarios for why she wasn't there. But then my rational mind kicked in and said *she's probably just outside taking a leak, chill out.* Yeah, that makes more sense than something necessarily being *wrong.* And then my rational mind and the other mind joined forces with a new argument: *She would have heard the car coming from down the street like she does, and definitely would have heard it turn into the driveway. She always gets so excited when anyone comes home that she would have bolted for the garage even in mid-pee.*

The garage door was fully lifted, and there was no Chloe.

Yep. Something was wrong.

Dad gave voice to it first. "Where's the dog?" Lilly finally stopped her yammering and leaned forward in her seat to get a better look out the windshield. Dad pulled the car in slowly just in case Chloe were to suddenly burst through the back-yard door and into the car's path. But she didn't. The door hung open, as it had been when we left. Snow fell just outside and a few flakes blew into the garage, melting almost as soon as they hit the concrete floor. I think all our eyes were on that opened door, expecting her to bound through, eyes bright and tongue lolling.

Dad put the car in park and shut off the engine.

"Where is she?" asked Lilly. Her jubilant tone had given way to one of steadily increasing panic.

We all exited the vehicle and Lilly was first to reach the backyard door. She stepped out into the dark night, the snow crunching and squeaking beneath her feet. "Chloe!" she called, her breath a cloud of white. "Come here, girl!"

No jangle of dog tags, no anxious whining.

I flipped on the outside light and stepped out into the yard. The snow-coated ground was bathed in halogen blue. Just beyond where we stood, a single path of disappearing dog prints marked the snow. They started at the backyard door and led out into the yard, eventually trailing beyond the reach of the light. The snowfall had covered any previous tracks like taking an eraser to them, and now only this one relatively fresh set remained. Chloe must have stayed inside the garage during most of the storm and had only recently been drawn out into it, leaving her prints behind, which were even now slowly fading.

Dad had been looking over my shoulder and we must have had the same thought at the same time because he disappeared to his workbench for a second and returned with a flashlight. With a click, the bright beam shot through the darkness. Together, we followed the prints, thick snowflakes cascading through the beam like a barrage of falling stars. By then, Mom and Soren were standing outside too, and they watched as Dad and I investigated this odd set of tracks that did not circle, wander, or deviate. Wherever Chloe had been going, she'd been focused and intent on getting there. But those tracks had an unnatural look to them for some reason, and I could not explain it. They were too...direct. Too straight. Too unlike Chloe.

The chill I felt could have been from the cold, it's true, but looking back, I think it was from something else.

Mom had been holding Lilly back by the shoulder, but she broke free and came scampering through the snow, her bright pink snow boots kicking up skiffs of powder.

"Lilly!" called Mom, but her daughter was already gone.

We followed the trail past the back patio where it quite suddenly veered to the right. We stopped. Lilly nearly crashed into me and reached out for my hand. I took it and her cold little fingers laced with mine. Dad shone the flashlight at the chain link fence separating the backyard from the field behind our house. Chloe's prints met up with the fence and then continued on the other side of it, extending far out into the field and into darkness.

"Aw, damn it," Dad muttered.

Snow had been collecting in the bottoms of the diamonds in the chain link fence but at the point where Chloe's tracks ended, the snow had been knocked away. Upon closer inspection, Dad found a tuft of black hair caught against a sharp edge in the fence. He pulled it free and sighed.

"She's loose," he called out to Mom. "Climbed the fence."

From the backyard door I heard Mom click her tongue and groan.

I felt Lilly's grip tighten and she looked up at me. The look in her enormous blue eyes nearly broke my heart. Snow had gathered atop her blonde head, and I reached out to brush it away.

"What could have made her jump the fence?" asked Mom.

Dad laughed, but it was humorless. "I don't know." Resigned, he clicked off the flashlight and turned to go back to the house.

Lilly let go of my hand and went after him. "We have to go find her right now!" she cried. I stared at the fence as the memory of how terrified Chloe had been of those firecrackers resurfaced, how desperate she'd been to escape. It hadn't been an easy climb, either, but so frantic had she been that, for her, it was either climb or die.

I wondered then what on earth could have driven her to do the same thing again. Nobody sets off fireworks in December around here, not even on New Year's Eve. There's pots and pans for that. The only thing that came to mind was gunfire, but to my knowledge, no one in the neighborhood made a habit of shooting off a round or two at random. I guess it was possible that someone had spotted a coyote or something and had shot to scare it away, but I just didn't think so. Besides, Chloe had heard the shot of a gun before when Dad took her hunting with him one autumn and she didn't freak then. "We're gonna go right now, right Dad?" Lilly continued as the two reached Mom and Soren at the garage.

"Yes, Lilly," said Dad. "You are staying here, though. Your brother and I will find her." I thought for sure Dad was referring to Soren and so didn't expect it when I heard him call for me to get in the truck. I turned and started across the yard toward the garage.

"Nooooo," whined Lilly, in that distraught way that begins high-pitched and slowly tumbles a good seven octaves. It was her trademark whine.

"Lilly, its cold outside and you need to get to bed," said Mom.

"She's my dog too. I'm going," declared Lilly, stomping into the garage and circling around to Dad's truck. She left behind white snow tracks in the shapes of her boot treads. "Besides, it's Friday and I don't have school tomorrow."

"Lilly Ann Patrick, if you—" Mom stopped as Lilly opened the passenger's side door and lifted herself into the cab of Dad's truck. With an indignant look on her face, Lilly slammed the door shut behind her. Mom turned to Dad slack-jawed with a *Can you believe her?* expression. Dad just shrugged.

"She gets it from you," he said.

Mom turned back to Lilly, who was doing her best to ignore anything on the other side of the windshield. Mom got her attention and then drew a finger across her throat with her tongue out, which, speaking from experience usually meant you were in big trouble and would certainly catch it later.

"I'll go get her thicker coat," Dad said. "Daniel, hop in with your sister."

We circled the block first, hoping to see Chloe scampering through a neighbor's yard or cowering beneath a deck. Any prints she may have left behind were now covered with fresh snow, so we had no hope of tracking her. We thought to knock upon the front doors of homes with lights still on in the hopes that someone might have seen her, but the only people who appeared at home and awake were the Tomlinsons. They were an elderly couple, both hard of hearing and both with terrible eyesight who wouldn't have seen her if she'd been painted neon and stood two inches from their noses. Dad always joked that one or both of them would one day go home with the wrong spouse after bingo night and not realize it until the next day, if at all. Their Christmas lights were still on and through their huge front window we could see their big Christmas tree glowing red from top to bottom. Of course, they'd had someone do their decorating for them, but at least they still cared to be festive for the season. We decided not to bother them, knowing better.

"She's probably freezing to death," said Lilly, who sat in the middle between Dad and me. The heater was blasting warm air on us, the wipers going at full speed to brush away the falling snow. With the streets snow-packed and visibly dangerous, Dad drove slowly and took the corners carefully. Collisions and other accidents would certainly be happening tonight but not in this neighborhood. No one but us was out in this storm. I rolled down the window periodically to call out Chloe's name, but the winter air stole the heat so quickly I never got out more than one or two good calls before needing to crank it back up.

I'd thought about the culvert right away but wanted to search the neighborhood first just in case. When I finally suggested it, Dad nodded and looked at me like I'd just solved an impossible riddle. Beside me, I could literally feel Lilly's spirits lift. Dad turned the truck around and we headed toward Maple Street.

The Goldammer Creek was only named so because the majority of it flowed through Gary and Bette Goldammer's land about two miles east of Maple Street, and truth be told, I think only the neighborhood kids called it that. I'm sure it had an official name (or maybe not) but that's how we'd always known it. It was a shallow ribbon of the clearest water you'd ever seen, twisting though the neighborhoods of our little town, and was home to water-skippers and tadpoles in the summer. In the winter, however, it was a ribbon of ice, frozen solid in time. From November through March, except for the rocks poking through the surface it was unblemished glass. In its voyage downstream, the creek coursed beneath only two streets in the whole town: Main Street and Maple Street. The Main Street conduit was, of course, a cement-reinforced pipeline that ensured absolute strength and durability. The Maple Street conduit was nothing more than a ribbed, metal culvert with a mouth as wide as the creek itself. I can remember many a summer afternoon playing deep within that culvert with my friends, pretending we were robbers hiding from the law or ghastly creatures borne from watery sludge with a taste for human blood.

We pulled off to the side of Maple Street right beneath a streetlight, and as far to the side as we could get, but with absolutely no traffic, Dad didn't think we were in much danger of being sideswiped.

"Lilly, stay in the truck. That's not up for negotiation," he said with absolute authority, something poor Mom lacked in her disciplining. It was that *absoluteness* that had always made us kids abide by his rules and commands over Mom's. Lilly didn't raise so much as a squeak of protest at Dad's orders, and I wondered right then if that was ever a bone of contention between Mom and Dad. He shifted the truck into neutral and depressed the emergency brake. "If you follow us, you're getting a real spanking, and I'm serious about that." He killed the engine and opened his door to a flurry of snowflakes. "Daniel, grab the flashlight and let's go have a look."

Maple Street served as a sort of bridge between subdivisions: the Raddock and ours. There were homes on the fringes, but along the creek there were only trees and acres of vacant grassland. The ground sloped down gently from the street to the creek bank, but covered in slippery wet snow, it was still slick as ice and Dad and I took baby steps, the bright yellow circle from the flashlight bouncing across our path. In the spring, you'd hear the soft gurgle of water coursing over rocks, but in winter, there was nothing but a chilly silence. All that could be heard was the crunch of snow underfoot, and our breathing.

We reached the creek bank and stepped through a barrier of dead brambles, their spindly stems gathering snow in heaps. There was almost no discerning where the land ended and the frozen creek began as both were hidden beneath the same fluffy white blanket, but inside the culvert the creek would no doubt be clear, solid black crystal.

Dad set his hand on the lip of the metal culvert to peer inside and quickly withdrew it with a hissy breath pulled in between clenched teeth.

"Shit's cold," he said, and then sort of chuckled. We both then stepped out onto the frozen creek and bent over to see inside the hollow.

In the daytime, you'd be able to see straight through the culvert, a wide circle of daylight on the other side. But tonight, it was only a black tunnel stretching into infinite dark, deep and without end. We could see in for about six feet or so from the splash of light provided by the streetlight, but beyond that was pitch black. The longer our eyes adjusted, the more we could vaguely see the other side where that same light spilled onto the opposite end of the creek, but mostly, that view was lost inside a veil of shadow.

"Chloe," I called, hoping that if she were inside, she'd hear my voice and come running, knowing whatever danger she'd feared had passed and it was safe to come out. "Chloe?" I swung the flashlight beam up and pointed it down the tunnel.

There was the sound of something moving around like the shifting of a rock or the cracking of ice, and it echoed out the culvert.

At first nothing appeared to move, and my flashlight beam jerked left and right, the circle of light touching ice and rocks and dead leaves that had blown in and gotten caught when the creek froze. Then about three-quarters of the way across, I saw a dog-sized clump of fur. And next to it, the mass I'd first dismissed as a wet, black rock, suddenly twitched. The rock twitched.

"Chloe?"

There was a strange tearing sound, followed by a stomach-turning gurgle, or a noise like the one made when you're drinking through a straw and finally reach the bottom of the glass. All my attention was on that dark clump of fur. I held my breath, hoping once that raccoon or possum or whatever-the-fuck-it-was moved out of the way, that clump of fur wouldn't turn out to be my dead dog. But then that raccoon or possum rose up, nearly doubling in size, and turned what served as its head and looked at Dad and me. And it certainly was no raccoon or possum. In fact, it was far from being any animal I'd ever seen. The flashlight caught its eyes for a mere second, and they flashed in that way that animal's eyes do—demonic and green.

But as quickly as it had risen, it took to its feet, turned, and sped without making a sound across the ice and out the opposite end of the culvert. I tried to follow it with the flashlight, the beam jerking and darting, but the whatever-it-was was far too fast, and it reached up with a strange, clawed hand

and pulled itself up out of the culvert. In two seconds flat, it had fled and was gone.

"What the fuck was that?" I asked, breathless.

"Language," was all Dad said. He grabbed the flashlight out of my hand and hunched down to enter the culvert.

"Dad," I said in protest, suddenly afraid. The thought of going *in* there, into where that whatever-it-was had just been and could easily return, filled me with a leaden terror I could not explain. Added to that, the possibility of seeing my dog, my Chloe, dead and devoured by some monstrous *thing* nearly made me want to scream. I was overcome by a paralyzing fear I'd never felt before. My feet were planted. I watched Dad's silhouette creep down the tunnel toward the dog-sized clump of fur, my guts churning. "Dad," I repeated but the only evidence was a white cloud from my mouth. My voice had disappeared.

Halfway in, Dad stopped and pointed the flashlight down. He knelt on his haunches. I heard him sigh and couldn't quite tell if it was in relief or despair. The light glided up and down the body of what could be my dead dog, and I felt my heart skip a beat.

"It's not Chloe," Dad said, his voice echoing out the culvert. "Looks like...well, it's not Chloe."

Air that had been trapped in my lungs was suddenly expelled in a great hiss of white, and with it, half of my fear. The other half remained, however, and I couldn't resist the urge to tell Dad to get his ass outta there.

We drove through town for the next hour, finding nothing, Lilly in tears. I instinctively never mentioned the thing, the whatever-it-was, in front of her, knowing it would only scare her and cause her to distress more than she already had. I'd save it for later. I could see in Dad's eyes as we continued our search that his mind was trying to work it out as well. A badger? Lynx? Yes, a lynx…some mutant, sludge-covered lynx. Because it was slick, slimy, not fur-coated. And it had claws. Lynxes have claws. But this thing didn't have ears like a lynx. Because it was a *mutant* lynx, of course.

Did we even have lynxes in Idaho?

Through Lilly's tearful disapproval, Dad called off the search until the next day. I helped reinforce his decision, saying how we'd never find Chloe in the dark, and she was probably nestled up beside someone's fireplace right now anyway. She had tags with our phone number and address on them and we'd undoubtedly be getting a call first thing in the morning. I'd hoped Lilly didn't detect an ounce of disbelief in my reasoning. Because it was there. Despite knowing we weren't coming any closer to finding Chloe that night, I wanted to balk at Dad for calling off the search too. I wanted my dog at home. Out of this cold. Safe. From everything.

When we got home Dad carried Lilly inside, her head resting on his shoulder, sobbing all the way to her bedroom. Dad laid her gently in her bed and closed the door. We didn't see him for twenty minutes, knowing he was doing his best to console and comfort, probably reading her a bedtime story like he used to. A quiet somberness had settled on the household.

"Dad."

I found him later, sitting at the desk in the tiny room that served as the office, lit by a small lamp with a green plastic shade. He was paying bills. The kind on paper, not online. Old habits die hard.

"Yes?"

I leaned against the doorway, stared at the back of his head. "What was that thing?"

He took a moment to answer. "It was some...animal, son."

"What kind of animal looks like that, Dad?"

He just shrugged his shoulders. "I'll call Henry over at Animal Control tomorrow. Let him know about it. They'll take care of that poor dead deer in the culvert, too. Help us locate Chloe."

My next question was not one I necessarily wanted a detailed answer for, and I debated asking it at all. But I felt like I had to know, *needed* to know, no matter how hard it might be to hear, thinking it might help solve the mystery of the what-ever-it-was. Dad felt my pause, sensed my reluctance, and turned in his chair, looking at me with eyebrows raised as if to say *Anything else? I'm busy here.*

"How...did the deer look?"

Dad's eyebrows fell and he turned back around. He picked up the pen and continued cutting checks.

"Bad."

And that was all he said.

After sharing a non-alcoholic eggnog with Mom, I bid the family goodnight and retired to my own bedroom.

I stripped to my boxer-briefs and crawled into bed. I hadn't bothered to close the blinds on my window and so had a clear view of the snow continuing its relentless descent. My mind swam with dark thoughts of Chloe: shivering, slowly freezing to death in some alleyway, terrified and lost, getting stolen, getting eaten by—

I turned onto my side, chased the thoughts away.

And then another thought crept in.

Firebug.

The first time I'd heard that word I was thirteen and thought my Government teacher was talking about those insects with the glowing butts you find during a Midwestern summer. I had no idea she was referring to me. She'd caught me flicking a lighter in class, staring transfixed at the silky flame, before snatching the lighter away, saying I knew the school rules. I got detention for it. She'd said it in passing, and I barely even registered it: *firebug*.

But it didn't officially become who I'd forever be known as around town until I was fifteen, the stupid nickname that would apparently become my legacy.

Mom and Dad had been separated for almost a year at that time. Mom was living across town with her parents and Lilly, while Dad and Soren and I carried on at the house. There were talks of reconciliation, mentions of Mom and Lilly coming back home, but nothing was concrete yet. Nothing settled. I was having trouble believing all the talk and had established myself comfortably within my new identity as a cynical, bitter teen, frequently telling Dad that "love was a bunch of shit," and "Why don't you just get divorced already?" Things like that. Yeah, I was a real ray of sunshine.

I would later learn that being in love is only a part of what makes marriage work, and love had not been the problem with my folks. Mom always said they were soulmates and she'd known it the night they'd met. She'd always loved him, would always love him, and if they could just figure out all the other bullshit, they'd be just fine. But all that other bullshit— Dad constantly escaping into his work, Mom's failure to communicate her needs, Dad's insensitivity, Mom's hypersensitivity—is what eventually led to the separation.

Neither had known it would be for as long as it was; Dad

thought Mom would be out of the house for a month, maybe two. But two months turned into three, which turned into four, which turned into the Earth's full rotation around the sun. I guess in a way I'd seen it coming. Mom cried a lot and Dad did a lot of useless tinkering with things in the garage. I remember once when I was eleven, they'd gotten in a big fight, and afterward Mom shut herself away in the bedroom and Dad said the coffeemaker needed fixing. I hadn't been aware it was broken; it seemed to have worked just fine at breakfast.

The night Daniel died and Firebug was born was a hot, dry night in August. The kind of night where you can still smell the cooked earth in the air well after the moon has replaced the scorching sun.

My buddy Nick had recently gotten his driver's license, and we'd spent the past month and a half tearing up the back-country roads in his dad's Ford pickup. It was the freest I'd ever felt; no adult supervision, just me and my friend (or friends, depending upon whom we could get scrunched in between us on the middle console) ripping up the dirt prairie roads, drinking stolen whiskey, and laughing until we cried.

Among a favorite of our adventures was discovering an old abandoned three-story house in the middle of a wheat field. We'd convinced ourselves it was haunted and went barking from floor to floor, tempting the ghosts to show themselves. Our friend, whom we affectionately referred to as Truffles (so named after the dance made famous by a character called Chunk from *The Goonies*), scolded us for provoking the restless spirits and said we'd deserve anything bad coming to us.

Still, he'd join us whenever we'd decide to go there and wreak some teenage havoc. We'd throw rocks through windows, piss on the warped hardwood floors, howl and cavort through every room, and generally revel in our horsing around. We particularly liked going at nighttime when it seemed way scarier. We liked the only light being the bouncing beams of our flashlights, and the thought of something translucent and ghoulish being around every darkened corner. And it made Truffles even more nervous. We *really* liked that.

On this night in August, Nick and I had picked up three of our other friends for an evening of adventure. Nick had once again stolen a bottle of Jack from his father's abundant liquor cabinet. Casey, because he was the smallest—weighing in at a measly 94 pounds—got to ride bitch in between Nick and I. Tyler, being the newest member of our group, was forced to ride in the bed along with Truffles, who wouldn't fit bitch even if we'd wanted him to.

The air was warm, and it blasted in on us through the opened windows, washing our bare-skinned torsos. Casey was testing his flashlight and it kept blinking out. He'd hit it with the palm of his hand, and it would flicker for an instant before dying.

"Dad keeps spare batteries in the glove box, dude," said Nick. "What's it take?"

"Nine-volt. Two of 'em."

"Danny…" said Nick, nodding at the glove compartment. I rummaged around the odd collection of round batteries, not finding the required square ones.

"What kind of flashlight takes nine-volts anyway?" I asked.

"This kind," said Casey proudly. "It's military-grade. My granddad gave it to me. Jealous?"

"No. Mine *works*," I said, flashing it on and off. Casey leaned against me hard, squishing me against the door.

"Hey!" I yelled, giggling, pushing him back. His shoulder slammed into Nick's.

"Watch it!" yelled Nick, "I'm driving here!"

I eventually found two nine-volts and handed them to Casey. Once inserted, he flicked the switch and a bright beam shot to the roof. With his mouth, he made the sound effect of a lightsaber coming to life. I turned my flashlight on in response, making the same sound effect. Before either one of us could spout an appropriate *Star Wars* quote, Nick intervened.

"Knock it off, nerds."

Casey replied by giving him a wet willy.

We crested a hill and suddenly the black outline of the tall house came into view. The truck headlights played across its chipped, faded blue side, illuminating bits and pieces, but only hinting at what it looked like in full light. From the truck bed, we heard a howl of delight. It must have been Tyler. Truffles would not have been so outwardly excited.

Nick steered the truck from one dirt road onto another and finally skidded to a dusty halt beside our house. We heard the boys in the back tumble forward, followed by a whiny "Ouch!" I looked over my shoulder and saw Truffles peeling his face off the back window. We leaped out of the cab into the warm night air, our T-shirts sticking out of our back pockets like horsetails.

The lofty house loomed in the darkness, utterly uninviting. But to five 15- and 16-year-olds, it was a playground. We barreled through the front door, each of us calling out "Honey, I'm home!" at the tops of our lungs. There was just something uniquely thrilling about being set loose within a house where someone once lived and reigning over it all. Masters of our domain. Free to be as destructive as we wanted. It was our right; we'd found the place, we'd staked our claim, and we made the rules. No parents, no adults. No fancy nice things to keep our feet off of or to wipe up if we made a mess. If we'd been a club, it would have been our clubhouse. There were a few furniture pieces left behind—a couch, a desk, a small dining table, a rolling shelf where perhaps a TV once sat—but mostly, it was free, empty space to run amok. And we did.

Nick uncapped the Jack and took a swig.

Casey was already taunting Truffles, dragging him upstairs, their flashlight beams zigzagging across the walls. "C'mon!" he squealed, his voice cracking, "I heard someone died in the upstairs bathroom! Hung themselves! Let's go have a look!" Not true, everyone including Truffles knew it wasn't true, and yet he groaned and gave the expression of deep concern often associated with feelings of genuine terror. He resisted a little, his meaty forearms pulling against Casey's birdlike claws, but it was futile. Casey broke into a laugh.

"Wait for me!" shouted Tyler, chasing up after them.

Nick and I shared the whiskey. He picked up a stone that had been thrown the last time we were here and threw it back outside through the last intact window in the living room. The glass shattered and fell to the floor in a dozen pieces.

"So, how're your parents?" he asked me.

I hesitated, not expecting that question from Nick. We usually stuck to topics like movies and music and girls. Rarely, if ever, did we venture into personal stuff, stuff that could potentially open up serious conversation about (gulp) feelings and (double gulp) real emotions. But sometimes there are moments with your buddies, moments when you get the opportunity to proclaim outright that you care about one another without irony or ego or embarrassment, and I felt that this was one of those moments.

"Um," I started, not sure how exactly to proceed, "Okay, I guess."

Not true. Everyone knows it's not true.

I sighed.

"Mom's still across town. But they're working things out, I guess. I dunno. It really sucks."

He handed me the bottle of Jack. I took a long drink and Nick squeezed my shoulder.

And that was it. But somehow, that was enough.

Seconds later we heard Truffles scream and a sound like elephants thundering down the stairs, elephants who'd apparently just played a hilarious joke.

This being Tyler's first visit to our house, we took the time to show him around, pointing out all the things we'd discovered and the things we'd inflicted. I did a little extra exploring of my own, opening drawers and cupboards I'd never opened before.

It was discovering the steel wool that put into motion every bad thing that followed.

Mom and Dad had long ago established the rule that if I were caught with fire-starting materials of any kind, I'd be grounded for six months. That, and worse. I think they'd never disclosed what the "and worse" would be because they liked the idea of the mysterious threat and the ability to make up whatever they wanted in order to hit me harder wherever I'd need it at the time. And to be fair, they had every right. I'd become somewhat of a hazard.

Dropping that flaming Kleenex into the wastebasket when I was twelve, seeing that beautiful warm dancing light, and being the *maker* of it, had awakened in me something deep, something stronger than mere fascination. Something akin to lust. I couldn't (and still can't) explain it. And I couldn't stop. I liked conducting little experiments in the backyard: what would happen if I lit a leaf on fire? A stick? A clump of dog hair? A few strands of my own hair? Any kind of food from the pantry (crackers, cereal, peanut butter, rice, nutmeg, sugar, flour)? Clothing? A grasshopper? The welcome mat? A weed in the garden? The garden?

Obviously, some things burned better and more magnificently than others and I quickly learned the most flammable materials. And I'd had constant access to fire-starters. Until I got busted by my Government teacher. And then the party was over. The end. Mom and Dad hid or did away with all the matchbooks and lighters in the house and swore that if they ever saw another sign that I'd been starting fires they'd ground me. And worse.

My friends refused to support my habit, knowing that it was: a) dangerous and wildly stupid; and b) would land me in the teenage slammer known as "being grounded" and I wouldn't be able to hang out. No one was ever particularly impressed by my fearless fire-starting, so I realized it was a special passion of mine and mine alone.

So while I couldn't get access to the convenient, conventional methods, there was such a thing as the Internet and I began googling ways to start fires without matches or lighters. And what a treasure trove of knowledge that crazy Internet was! I only ever once used one of the methods I learned (the fire plough technique, which was a lot of work) and only attempted another (the beaming-the-sun's-rays-through-a-magnifying glass technique, which took a while, but was cool as hell), but the ways in which I could give birth to that seductive, hypnotic being (for that was what it started to become for me—a sentient being, as alive as you or I) were many, and I never felt completely cut off from it, despite the absence of my conventional methods of bringing it to life.

And there was one other way. A way so simple, I'd never tried it because I feared what it could do. What it would do to me. *For* me. But the cocktail of elements that composed that particular night were enough to make my lust completely irresistible.

And I'd found that steel wool.

It was beneath where the kitchen sink would have been if there'd been a kitchen sink. Three individually wrapped packages. Never been used. The *fine* steel wool too, not the coarse kind.

I gently pulled apart the cellophane and withdrew the pad that was oddly both soft and sharp. I squeezed it.

"Casey," I called out, "come 'ere."

A warm, gentle breeze blew in through the broken window above the sink area. The dry, moth-eaten curtains hugging the frame billowed and waved peacefully like two hovering ghosts. I waited a second before calling out again, feeling as if Casey's lack of response was perhaps a warning from some higher force: *This is your last chance to rethink what you're about to do. You can change your mind in an instant.* But as I didn't much believe in higher forces or anything having to do with the supernatural back then, I ignored that potential warning and called out again.

"Casey!"

I heard him from the other room. "What!"

"Come here, I wanna show you something!"

For a little guy, he sounded like he must have heavy cement blocks for feet, the way he tromped down the hallway and into the kitchen. He held his flashlight under his chin so the beam shone right up his nostrils. He was making a face.

"Wow, that's a better look for you," I said.

"You think?" He bucked his front teeth way out and crossed his eyes. Sharp shadows carved deep trenches in his face and he looked like a Halloween jack-o-lantern. "How about this?"

"Oh, *way* better," I said. "Now if we could only make it stick that way you might just get a girlfriend."

Casey lowered his voice, raked his mop of blonde hair over his eyes. "Will you go out wiff me, pwease? I'm so wonewy and no one will tawk to me."

This made me laugh pretty hard. I almost forgot what was in my hand until Casey asked, "What's that?"

"Gimme your flashlight."

"You have your own."

"Just give it to me."

He handed it over with about as much enthusiasm as a small child relinquishing a lollipop. I began unscrewing the end of the casing and he exclaimed in the same childish way. "Hey, what are you doing?"

"Don't throw a fit, I just wanna show you something cool."

I pulled the end of the casing off and detached the 9-volt battery from the contact wires. With a battery in one hand and the steel wool in the other, I grinned excitedly at Casey. His brow wrinkled but I could see the curiosity in his eyes. The warm breeze returned, filling out the ragged curtains, causing them to bulge and then deflate as the wind escaped out the sides. *This is your last chance…*

"Watch."

I brought the objects in my hands together. With two vigorous swipes, the friction between the battery's contacts and the steel wool set loose several little orange sparks that slid up the length of the metal shavings. Casey gasped. The smoldering died slowly, but I could see the wonder in Casey's eyes as if I'd just shown him a magic trick, and I did it again, this time with five or six vigorous swipes. I could feel the heat conducting through the wool, but it didn't sting enough for me to let go. The smoldering was brighter this time, and a few sparks jumped the wool and into the air. It was beautiful, like holding my own little apple-sized version of the Fourth of July.

And what I did next came from a desire to fan the flames (no pun intended) of Casey's wonderment because the look on his face sent a thrill through me. It was a look that I always imagined I had whenever that hypnotic, mysterious element was at my fingertips, mine to control and admire, a look that told me for once, for *once*, someone is sharing this sensation with me. They're sharing it with me. That odd feeling of being possessed by lust and unable to stop was also pushing forward and suddenly I had to see it. I had to. It didn't even seem like the wrong thing to do. So I did it.

From the corner of my eye, I saw Casey's expression change, but it was too late. He knew what I meant to do. I rubbed the battery against the wool a few more times, just to keep that beautiful apple-sized Fourth of July ignited and glowing, and I held the wool against the dry, brittle curtain hugging the right side of the kitchen window.

The kindling was effortless. Blue at first, then an orange so bright it was almost red. The small flame whipped upward, gaining its footing, realizing it had been called into existence, and then quickly went to work. It slithered up the curtain like a serpent through grass and before I'd known what I'd done, began licking the ceiling.

"OhshitDaniel," was all one word as Casey took three stumbling steps backwards.

I dropped the wool to the floor and it smoldered for a few seconds, the sparks gliding along the metal threads like lit fuses before blinking out.

The spot where the tip of the flame brushed against the ceiling was instantly blackened, and then a separate tendril of fire crawled across the curtain rod, eating that delicious cloth tinder, and spread down to the other curtain. It happened so fast. And now I was beginning to realize what I'd unleashed. The realization crept slowly, nothing like the speed at which the fire was devouring the curtains and spreading to the wall and ceiling. Wallpaper was peeling and something within the wood was hissing. And then I knew what I'd done could not be easily undone. The fire was hungry, *starved*, consuming at a pace that I'd never seen before. I was captivated.

"What's that smell?" shouted Tyler. He and the others were upstairs sharing the Jack when suddenly a loud clamoring of three boys down the steps drowned out the crackling and hissing from the growing fire in the kitchen. Nick came around the corner and immediately knew.

"Daniel!"

Casey turned and fled the kitchen, which was beginning to fill with black smoke. He joined the other boys standing at the foot of the stairs. A light bulb in the chintzy kitchen light fixture burst with a tinkling of glass. The fire, which had spread to resemble a wind-kissed rippling blue lake boiled over my head.

"Daniel!"

What was before a crackle and a hiss was turning into a deep growl. And the heat was nearly overwhelming. I could feel it on my bare chest, on my cheeks. I suddenly imagined my hair catching fire, which judging from the flames that were now blanketing the ceiling directly above my head, was a very real possibility. I marveled at the sight of it all, felt a sense of pride at having been the cause of it, but also a sense of fear. This was no wastebasket fire. This was no backyard experiment I could easily throw a cup of water on and extinguish. And then, *then* the meaning of what I'd done hit me.

It's out of my control.

I made it and now it's out of my control.

"Daniel, goddammit!"

I backed out of the kitchen toward the others. Someone, probably Nick, grabbed my arm with a grip like a vice and yanked me away so hard I felt the bones in my neck crack.

"See, I told you guys," Truffles shrieked. "I told you bad things would happen!"

"This wasn't ghosts, you idiot," said Nick, rushing me through the house like an angry father. "It was Daniel."

Coughing our lungs to shreds, we poured out the front door.

"Let's go, let's get out of here!" shouted Tyler between hacks. Black smoke flowed from the house's broken windows. The moonlit sky was quickly turning charcoal gray, the stars blocked from our view.

"Why'd you do it, Daniel, why?" shouted Nick. He was

leading me toward the pick-up. I twisted out of his grasp and stopped.

"What are you, my dad?" I said angrily.

"What are you talking about?"

"I just wanted to show Casey a trick, that's all!"

"No, that's not all!"

Tyler leapt into the bed of the pick-up. "Who cares, let's go!"

Casey stood staring dumbly at the house. I couldn't tell if it was in shock or in awe. Or perhaps in a sort of terror.

"Casey, get in the truck!" yelled Nick. Casey snapped out of his hypnosis and followed Nick's orders, his T-shirt whipping the backs of his knees as he ran. He gave me a quick look before jumping into the cab, a look that drove this shameful reality into my bones.

What have you done?

I turned away from my friends and back to the house, my eyes eager to see how the fire had spread. Sharp hints of orange were teasing out the windows like the claws of some beast trying to dig its way up. Glass shattered. A fizzing sound was layered beneath the growl, and I could see the paint on the wood panels bubbling and blistering. And then something exploded (or collapsed) and the fire suddenly took a giant breath, increasing in size.

"Dan, let's go!" yelled Nick. He grabbed for my wrist. I shook him off. "What are you doing, let's get out of here before we get caught!" I think he continued yelling, saying things like *pyromaniac* and *huge trouble* and *wheat field*. Maybe *brush fire* or *forest fire* or something. But I heard none of it. I was locked in. Despite the shame and the fear I'd felt seconds ago, I was now completely spellbound.

The power of it. The *size* of it. And the beauty.

Most of all, that strange, sentient beauty.

The next thing I was aware of was the slamming of two truck doors and the revving of an engine. Taillights painted the dirt road red. Tires kicked up dust. Truffles's face stared after me, forlorn and apologetic, from the back of the pickup speeding away from me.

They'd left me alone out here. Stranded, with this (my, our) burning house. Strangely, I didn't much care.

I decided to have a seat.

Might as well enjoy the show.

Even several yards back I could still feel the immense heat coming from the house. Sweat ran down my chest and I could feel it trickling down my back. I pulled my T-shirt out of my back pocket, mopped up the perspiration, and slung it over my shoulder. I relaxed back onto my elbows, watching the house burn as if I were watching a TV show in my living room.

As the flames began forming an impenetrable shell of destructive orange around the house, a word popped into my mind, *the* word, the word that I so often thought about when I watched things burn. The word before *firebug*.

Raze.

As in "raze the house to the ground."

Though, when I'd first heard the phrase, I'd thought it looked like this: "*raise* the house to the ground." And that never made sense to me. Raise? As in "lift up"? How do you lift something up to the ground? So, I looked it up in the ol' Merriam-Webster Dictionary. And lo and behold, it was spelled r-a-z-e. Raze. Definition #1: erase. To scrape, cut, or shave off. Definition #2: to destroy to the ground. And I thought it funny how two opposing words are spelled differently but are pronounced exactly the same. And "raze" rhymed with "blaze," which amused me. Ah, the English language.

So, from then on, "raze" became my word. To destroy. Yes, fire was beautiful and ancient and mysterious and somehow intelligent, and it was all those things that intrigued me, but it was also the destructive power of it. The power to melt, to reduce to ashes, to completely transform one thing into another. To annihilate.

Sitting there, propped up on my elbows and watching the house burn, it was that which excited me the most. I'd annihilated our house. Killed it. Murdered it. This odd, dark sense of pride and power washed over me, despite the other feelings I felt (shame, regret, the fear of consequence). In that moment, I'd summoned forth the mightiest power known to man to do my bidding, and it kindly obliged. I was like Zeus— "Release the Kraken!" No, I was like Prometheus, giving fire as a gift to all mankind! For shouldn't everyone feel the way I did? Shouldn't they marvel and worship this force that can create even as it destroys? Might something unexpected and incredible come out of razing this house to the ground? It happens with forest fires all the time. Certain seeds can only open when enough heat—heat from a fire—prompts them to germinate. And so, in that moment I also felt like a creator. Some new thing would take the place of this house (which was nothing less than a fireball at that point) and I was the one who allowed it. Destroyer, creator. Me. A god.

An hour later, when the burning of the house had reached its spectacular climax, the fire trucks and police cars arrived. They found me leaning back in the same position I'd been in for most of the show. And right behind them came my parents. My first thought was of how great it was to see the two of them arrive in the same car together. It lifted my heart in a way watching the house burn never could. But once as a team they brought the hammer down, that feeling quickly went away.

I was lucky—really fucking lucky—to not have started the farmer's wheat field on fire, the same farmer who owned the house. It may have been vacant, but not abandoned. The farmer didn't press charges (because he gave in to my parents' desperate pleading), which was also fucking lucky, and my worst punishment was having to go into therapy for twelve months, also during which I was forbidden to see any of my friends outside of school.

So basically, I was grounded for a year, which to a fifteen-year-old is an eternity. In that time, I lost most of my friends, Nick included. That was the downside. The upside was Mom and Dad finally figured their separation was contributing to my delinquency and so expedited their reconciliation. It was bound to happen anyway. They were made for each other, after all. And all it took was me burning down a house to bring them to their senses.

Word spread (like wildfire) through the town of what I'd done. In hindsight, I think Mom and Dad had it worse than me. They'd already known their struggling marriage was the topic of conversation around many a dinner table, and now they were also the horrible parents of a pyromaniac son. Imagine what scandalous talk that was generating! *"I blame the father, fathers are supposed to dole out the discipline and rule with a firm hand." "I blame the mother, she coddled the boy too much." "Why do you suppose he did it?" "I think he's got a mental disorder." "Well, if the parents hadn't separated for as long as they did, this never would have happened." "It all starts with the parents." "Shame on them."*

Yeah. Fuck Ferdinand.

My therapist asked me if I felt bad for what I'd done. I told him yes, because I honestly did. What I didn't tell him is that I didn't feel bad about burning down someone's house, nearly burning an entire wheat field, which was someone's livelihood. That house was ours, mine and Nick's and Truffles's and Casey's and it was just sitting there. No one really needed it, no one but *us*. And the wheat field hadn't caught fire, so no point in thinking *What if's*.

It wasn't until after Mom and Dad had taken me home that night that I felt bad about what I'd done. Because they'd looked at me like they didn't know me. I was like a stranger who'd wandered in off the street, not their son, not the product of their combined DNA, not the boy they'd created and raised for the past fifteen years. I was someone they didn't recognize at all. They didn't say how mad they were, they didn't say *"What were you thinking?"* They just shook their heads at this stranger in front of them, looking sad somehow, like I'd failed them in some monumental way and it broke their hearts, and said how *disappointed* they were. As if I'd suddenly destroyed their hopes and dreams of me ever being a good person, being a respectable, upstanding all-American boy who would one day turn into a respectable man with an honest job and a beautiful wife and perfectly model family.

I'd let them down so unfathomably that they hated themselves as parents and wondered what business they ever had in procreating. Getting slapped across the face wouldn't have stung more. I'd disappointed them. Them with their eyes that regarded me as an outsider.

Because I was. In that moment, I was.

The snow continued to drop even as I fell asleep that night, burying us deep and deeper. Dreams were dismal nightmares about Chloe and death and wildfires and strange creatures. It was not a good night for sleep.

CHAPTER THREE

Morning stabbed my eyes with an ultraviolet lance. The sun was bright and white and shone unpleasantly through my window, the sky the purest shade of blue I'd ever seen. The storm had finally passed, leaving behind the gift of a gorgeous December morning in recompense. But I knew what it meant for me: driveway detail. I'd no doubt be shoveling until my back ached and my muscles burned.

Walking into the kitchen for a cup of coffee I found Dad on the phone with Henry over at Animal Control, Mom at the dining table sharing a grapefruit with Soren, and Lilly staring woefully out the living room window. The glowing lights from the Christmas tree reflected off her blonde hair in kaleido-scopic blue and red and green.

"Morning," I said in a scratchy voice.

Lilly turned from the window. "Chloe still hasn't come home, Dan," she said. The despair in her voice and the glassy look in her eyes made my heart break. I was worried about our dog plenty, but seeing the desperation, the suffering on my sister's face was almost worse than Chloe's vanishing. She was the agony of loss incarnate.

I approached her at the window and kissed the top of her rainbow head.

"We'll find her, Lil. Don't worry."

I ate a quick breakfast, grabbed my iPod, threw on my coat, scarf, and gloves and grabbed the shovel from the garage. As I took off up the street to my first job, Dad and Soren pulled out of the driveway to meet up with Henry and continue the search for our dog. I don't know why, but right then I felt an uncomfortably sharp tingle in my belly, the kind you get when true fear is realized in a split-second, and it spreads up to your chest and takes your breath away.

Right then I doubted my own words to Lilly. I imagined Dad finding Chloe dead. I imagined that first night without her, and then Christmas morning without her. I imagined our lives marching relentlessly forward while dragging the heavy chains of grief behind us through every day. It would feel as if we'd lost a family member. It *would* be losing a family member.

My first stop was the Tomlinson's with their bright red Christmas tree standing radiantly in the window like a flaming pyre. Mrs. Tomlinson greeted me on the porch with a steaming cup of coffee and a croissant, which I accepted even though I'd already had my fill of caffeine and baked pastries for the day. She told me how fine I was looking, a comment which only served to reinforce her near blindness. But I was polite and said, "Thanks, you too," at which she scoffed, waved her hand in a *Shoo, go away!* gesture, and broke into a shy little giggle.

"Edie, get in here, you're not wearing a coat!" called Mr.

Tomlinson from a cracked window. My only thought as she shuffled back to the house was *It's amazing he could see that far to tell.*

The Tomlinson job (which included the sidewalk) took about 30 minutes and then I was on to the next house. By the time I was halfway finished a new mass of storm clouds had started to gather in the distance.

I groaned.

With three houses down and three to go, I decided to take a little break and head home to warm up for a bit. Dad's truck wasn't in the garage, which meant he and Soren still had not found Chloe. The tiniest bit of hope I'd allowed myself to feel on my walk home melted away.

I propped the shovel up against the wall and was turning off my iPod when something on the bottom of the opened garage door caught my eye.

I lowered it to have a closer look.

At first, I assumed it was splatters of mud somehow left behind by the car tires, or perhaps even Chloe digging at the bottom of the door in an attempt to escape whatever it was that had spooked her off. But upon further inspection, the marks proved to be neither mud nor made by anything I could possibly guess.

They were handprints. More specifically, *claw* prints. Claws with only three fingers. It appeared as though whatever had left these behind had slid its hands beneath the garage door from the outside in an effort to lift it. And get *in*side.

I ran a finger across the prints, expecting to make a streak through them because they truly looked *burned* onto the metal, which normally would have left behind some carbon. My finger came away clean. The substance was tacky, sticky, like dried black syrup. Not like carbon in the least bit.

"What…the fuck…" I heard myself say aloud.

I'd definitely show Dad when he got home. Something was telling me these were made by that *it* we saw in the culvert last night, and *it* had been responsible for scaring Chloe off into the night.

Made by no raccoon, possum, or mutant lynx.

Mom, busy in the office with her accounting work, was nice enough to take a break to make me lunch.

"Sandwich?" she asked.

"Grilled cheese?" I optioned.

"You got it."

"Crusts cut off?"

"Don't push your luck. And by the way, you're nineteen for God's sake."

I leaned against the counter with a nearly empty bag of potato chips, cramming the rubble into my mouth while Mom stood at the stove. The grilled cheese hissed on the skillet.

I made sure Lilly was nowhere around before asking my next question. Mom told me she was in the backyard building a snowman, an activity Mom had suggested to occupy her daughter's worried mind.

"Mom," I started. "Why did I stop believing in Santa Claus, do you remember?"

"Hmm…I think because you just got old enough to see through the fairy tale. It didn't make logical sense to you anymore."

"What, the delivering gifts to every child in the world in one night part?"

"Yes, that, and the squeezing down the chimney part, and

64

the 'What about people who don't *have* chimneys?' part, and toy-making elves and flying reindeer...all of it. You grew up. You grew smarter. It was sad, actually." Mom chuckled. "Your dad and I were so glad we still had Soren and Lilly to believe, but...it was sad watching the magical part of Christmas leave your world."

"Was Santa first, then the Easter Bunny and the Tooth Fairy and all that?" I asked.

Mom nodded. "Yeah, Santa started this domino effect. You don't remember?"

I shook my head, packing another grip of broken chips into my mouth.

"Every imaginative, impossible thing you thought to be true you began to question, because, well, you got wise enough to know it's *impossible*! Rabbits hiding colored eggs, a tooth-collecting fairy... The fact that she was a tooth-collector was inconsequential; she was a *fairy* for God's sake. You knew the world well enough by that point to know that fairies only existed in books and movies. I'm sure if we'd been churchgoing, God-fearing folk you'd have started questioning Jesus and the Bible too."

"Mom, you're pretty smart, right?"

"Well thanks for noticing, you tell your father that when he gets home."

"No, I'm serious. You're an intelligent human being."

"By certain standards, maybe."

"Was there ever a time in your life you stopped to reconsider what you believed to be possible?"

"What's with the existentialism all of a sudden?"

"Mom..."

"Yes."

"When?"

"When I came back to your father."

She stared at me hard and frankly. The grilled cheese sizzled.

We'd never had a conversation like this before.

"Why, Daniel?" she asked, flipping the sandwich. "Are you rethinking some...fundamental belief systems?"

"Just curious is all."

"What's going on in your noggin?"

"Nothing."

"Does this have to do with your drinking?"

I blushed. "No."

"With the fires?"

This time, I looked at her hard and frankly.

"No, Mom. I was just curious."

"You can talk to me, you know."

"I know."

And I did know. Just not about this.

Not yet.

The second half of Neighborhood Driveway Detail seemed to take just under a millennium. The temperature was steadily dropping and no longer could coat nor scarf nor gloves withstand the cold, so I decided enough was enough. I was nearly done with the last driveway and still had the sidewalk to do, but figured ah, fuck it. Its gonna snow tonight and I'm gonna have to do it all over again tomorrow. And besides, it's 4:30 and already dark.

Ugh. Northern winters.

I removed the glove from my stiff right hand, grabbed my

iPod and selected "Mr. Blue Sky" to play me home. Sometimes irony is the only appropriate combatant.

I slung the shovel over my shoulder like a hobo packing his wares and began my freezing march home. Great pockets of shadow occupied space beneath this pine tree, or that deck, or this elderberry bush, and I imagined Chloe springing from any one of these shadows to greet me with a torpedo nose to the crotch and a slobbery kiss. It didn't happen. And then I imagined the *it,* the *thing*…and *that* springing from the shadows…

I quickened my pace.

At that point, all I really had to be afraid of was an idea. A suggestion. One strong enough to get the ball of yarn unraveling, but really nothing more than an essence of what could be out there.

The following fifteen minutes changed all of that.

I was passing the Tomlinson's place and for the second time that day, noticed something odd. Something was different about their big front window. Something missing.

The bright red tree.

Strangely, there was still the red glow. However, now it was shining up from the floor like the carpet had caught fire.

I stopped "Mr. Blue Sky" and headed up their walkway to investigate.

No smoke. It's not a fire.

But the window's broken.

That's bad.

As soon as I got close enough to see both the Christmas tree and Mr. Tomlinson lying on the floor, all hesitation left me and I ran through the front door.

The scene I came upon was this:

The Christmas tree, still plugged into the wall but now

less a festive holiday symbol and more a glowing red and dark green snare, lay across Mr. Tomlinson's legs. Mr. Tomlinson lay on his back with the cordless telephone inches from his outstretched right hand. Blood painted a spot just above his right eye, which, along with the left, was closed. Other than the red lights from the tree, the room was entirely dark.

OhGodpleasedonotbedeadpleasedonotbedead…

I realized I'd frozen in fear for about ten seconds before shaking it off and rushing to Mr. Tomlinson's side.

My knees hit the floor beside him.

"Mr. Tomlinson?" I said, gently shaking him. "Mr. Tomlinson?"

He groaned, moved his head. I could see him trying to open his eyes, the flutter of those delicate, thin eyelids.

He tried to speak. I leaned in close.

"Edie…" he moaned. "Edie…"

With great effort he peeled his eyes open, blinked. Some sort of coherence came back to him suddenly and he looked at me with terror.

"Edie, my Edie…upstairs…she's upstairs."

That was my cue.

I stood and stumbled around in the dark frantically until my searching fingers found the handrail, and I didn't just run up the stairs—I *bounded* up them.

A tiny nightlight illuminated a small corner of their bedroom, but it was enough for me to see Mrs. Tomlinson, who sat on the floor, her back against the wall.

Her eyes were locked dead ahead. She was clutching rosary beads.

"Mrs. Tomlinson, are you alright?"

No answer.

I knelt next to her, catching my breath.

"Mrs. Tomlinson…"

She was also catching her breath.

I reached out and touched her shoulder. At this, she flinched, turned her head and finally acknowledged my presence. Her labored breathing continued, her knuckles turning white from her increasing grip on the rosary. The loose skin beneath her chin quivered.

"Mrs. Tomlinson…what happened?"

She stared at me through those milky cataracts. Her lip trembled. I thought for sure she was either going to burst into tears or throw up on me.

"It's inside…"

It was one of those times when I'd heard perfectly clear but for some reason, needed to hear it again. "What?"

Her words, though barely over a whisper, took on a crisp, urgent clarity.

"It's…in…side."

At that my blood went cold. My scalp prickled. There was no doubt who—or what—she was talking about. Immediately I began scanning the room for a possible weapon, any object to use in defense—

--small bedside lamp

--Mrs. Tomlinson's jewelry box

--picture frame

--glass of water

--Precious Moments figurine (grandma cuddling grandchild)

--another bedside lamp

--skinny vase in the corner

--books

--crap

--more crap

Thump. Thump-thump. From another room down the hall. And close by.

Mrs. Tomlinson gasped, pushing the rosary into her chest.

Skinny vase in the corner it is.

As quietly as I could, I stood up and stepped to the corner of the room. Tacky plastic cattails and other fake foliage plumed from the opening in the vase, and I quickly upturned it and dumped it all to the floor. It was thick blown glass, and slim enough at the bottom for me to brandish like a baseball bat, or a hatchet, like some kind of axe-wielding murderer, depending on your imagination. Mrs. Tomlinson made like she was about to speak, but I put a finger to my lips.

And that's when there was a *pop!* that elicited a squeal from Mrs. Tomlinson akin to a strangled goose, and an infinite darkness enveloped us. The nightlight was out, and the red glow from the Christmas tree downstairs was no longer warming the staircase. I could hear the blood rushing through my skull, feel every beat of my heart in my chest like the steadily increasing knock of a fist on an unanswered door, and I knew right then and there that I'd stumbled into the perfectly plotted cliché of a horror movie. Power's out. Monster in the house. Only me with my trusty vase for protection.

"Do you smell that?" Mrs. Tomlinson whispered.

I did. It was a smell I was more than a little acquainted with.

Burning.

My eyes had half-adjusted to the dark, which was just enough for me to stick my head out of the bedroom for a peek. Hallway: clear. But out of my periphery I caught a fleeing shadow sweep down the staircase. Which meant there was a new light source to cast said shadow. A warm, orange light source.

I swallowed hard and it clicked in my throat. I took a deep breath and exited the bedroom.

"Daniel…" pleaded Mrs. Tomlinson. I ignored her.

My descent down the staircase I now consider one of the bravest (and stupidest) things I've ever done. Against all my internal signals screaming at me to *RUN! RUN AWAY! AWAY=SAFE,* I continued forward like some lionhearted warrior entering a cave to slay the dragon. Something was down there, some *thing*, and I was about to face it, somehow *needed* to face it. The fear I felt was a strange thing; it lasted for four, maybe five seconds, and then was replaced by an even stranger sense of duty, responsibility, a practical *levelheadedness* even. My palms, however, were still sweating so profusely I had to reestablish my grip on the vase several times. I set foot on the last step and from here could see a motionless shadow. It could be Mr. Tomlinson's, or it could be the other thing. My last brave step around the corner would reveal the answer; I held my breath, flexed my grip on the vase, and took it.

The first thing my eyes registered was the Christmas tree on fire. It was a small flame, but inch-by-inch growing. Next was Mr. Tomlinson. He'd managed to dislodge his lower body somehow and was doing a laborious Army crawl away from the tree and toward the kitchen, cordless phone in hand. Last was the shadow caster. And here is where the ball of yarn blew completely apart.

It crouched, back to me, and was staring at the tree on fire. *Presumably* staring. I hadn't seen eyes yet, but I could only assume, based on my knowledge of living things, that it had eyes, and I remembered how they'd glowed like a cat's when Dad had shone the flashlight on it. At first it didn't move, but when it finally did, the appearance of this *it* took all my knowledge of carbon-based life forms and tossed it in the garbage. What it did, how it moved, defied the laws of physics. It just wasn't possible. *It* being here just wasn't possible. Yet here *it* was.

What I'd at first thought had been ears in the culvert, mutant lynx ears, was actually the *thing's* head *evaporating*. I can't think of a better word for it. It happened slowly, the edges of the "head" rising up, like horns, turning translucent like smoke. Then the rest of the head, the solid matter that *made up* the head, began to come undone, vaporizing into the air. With a quick jerk, the *thing* dipped its head to the ground, touched the carpeted floor and restored *it*self, arresting the slow disintegration. But then the "shoulders" started doing the same thing—evaporating like cold puddles on warm asphalt. It shifted its position a little, revealing its limbs—two arms, two legs—and the appearance brought to mind that of a common three-toed sloth, though far more skeletal. It slowly lifted a willowy arm and the sight of it made me shudder with a sick-stomach terror akin to finding a spider crawling up your shoulder. Suddenly quite afraid, I silently ducked back behind the corner, but my curiosity eventually got the better of me and I was peering back into the living room, watching the *thing* in rapt, horrified fascination.

It extended this long, insectile arm with four arched claws toward the flame as if it meant to touch it. I waited for the inevitable recoil once it felt the burn, but before that could happen, the claws became insubstantial, came apart and began drifting into the air. The smoky material that was becoming this creature's hand and arm mingled with the orange flame painlessly. It made a swirling motion with its vaporous hand like it was stirring the fire, and I was struck with the queerest thought: "It's *playing* with it…"

Then all at once, when it seemed more than half the creature's body had turned to smoke, it finally embraced the suspension and became more a ghost than a thing of solid matter. With animal-like swiftness it whipped to the other side of the burning Christmas tree as if desiring to see it from a different angle. Its gaseous body flattened to the floor and rose solid again, its glowing eyes now pointed in my direction. I gasped, sure I'd fallen into its line of sight, and pulled my head back. When I heard no sounds of pursuit, I carefully chanced another glimpse. The fire had eaten up the top branches and was now creeping down the trunk, and by this light I had my first clear view at the creature's face.

What popped into my mind right away was *The Scream*, that painting by Edvard Munch. Hairless and smooth, it looked more like a skull than a flesh-covered face. Its eyes were glowing orange dots as they reflected the firelight, its nose simply two bean-shaped holes in the center of its head. And its mouth was in that *Scream*-esque "O" shape, stretched and yawning. I had the distinct thought that this image was now branded into my mind and would undoubtedly be giving me nightmares in the weeks, months, possibly years to come. But still, I couldn't look away. There was something about the way it was exploring the fire, some eerily familiar look in its strange eyes, as if it had never seen this beautiful, wild spirit, this dancing light, and was completely enchanted by it. It was the same look that Casey had when I showed him my steel wool trick. Only more. Probably closer to what my *own* expression must've been like.

What followed was a strange waltz between the creature and the fire, the two at times inseparable, co-mingling and twisting together like lovers. Periodically, it tapped the wall with a "finger," connected with the floor, touched its head to the tree in these quick, almost involuntary movements to regain its solidity, as if fighting disintegration was a constant battle and connecting with something solid and firm stopped it. But like all dances, it was made to end, and was abruptly cut short by the shrill electronic ring of the smoke detectors.

Through the flames I saw its head snap up, and this time, I was sure that it saw me. I didn't even bother to duck behind the wall. For the briefest moment, we stared at each other, frozen in our shocked awareness of each other, both undoubtedly wondering if the other would make a move. The piercing squeal of the smoke detector continued, but neither of us seemed affected by it, so momentarily locked in as we were. When it blended with the approaching sound of sirens followed by a set of headlights suddenly sweeping across the wall, the trance was broken and the monster finally came for me. My heart leapt into my mouth at the speed with which it spider-crawled up the wall, this time defying the laws of gravity, and scrabbled in my direction. I readied the vase (Jesus, how stupid) and could only hope I wouldn't close my eyes in fear at the moment I needed to swing.

And yet, I did.

But swinging hadn't been necessary. The last thing I saw was the nimble, dark figure a foot away, and then upon opening my eyes, that figure crashed through a window in the kitchen behind me. As the shattered glass tinkled to the tiled floor, a fireman broke the front door open and charged inside with another fireman directly behind him, both donning masks and all as if they were barreling into a full-blown structure fire. One carried a red fire extinguisher, the other hefted a hose, both prepared for whatever level of fire dousing would be required. Blue and red lights swirled around the room. Fireman One pointed the extinguisher at the Christmas tree and let loose a spray of white foam while the other tossed aside the hose and flew to Mr. Tomlinson. He lifted the old man off the ground and took him outside as Officer Tackett (whom as kids we'd referred to as Officer Whack-It) entered the house. Our eyes met and my stomach dropped; Whack-It had been the officer on the scene when I'd torched the farmer's house.

It took Tackett a couple seconds to register it was me but once he did, his face reddened and his lips clenched together so tight they turned white.

"Dan Patrick, what are you doing here?" he spat.

"Mrs. Tomlinson is upstairs. She's okay but—"

Whack-It charged forward, pulling a pair of handcuffs off his belt and before I could do any more explaining, his big hands whirled me around.

"Wait a minute—" I said, my arms forced behind my back. The cold metal of the cuffs clasped painfully around both my wrists.

"Glen!" called Mrs. Tomlinson from upstairs. "Glen, what's happening down there?"

"Stay put, Mrs. Tomlinson," said Whack-It in his best TV cop voice. "Are you injured?"

"I'm fine but my heart is beating like a washing machine on the spin cycle. Is that you, Arnie? How's my Glen?"

The handcuffs cut into my bones, but my wincing had no effect on Whack-It's sympathies. He took me by the shoulder and ushered me past Fireman One and into the freezing night, driving me in the direction of his cop car. The strobing red-and-blue lights had a dizzying effect, and for a few seconds I had a feeling of complete unreality: this entire night is nothing more than a bad dream and I will soon wake up in twisted sheets with sweat-soaked hair.

But that didn't happen. The back door of the cop car flew open and a hand grabbed the top of my head.

"I didn't do anything! I was just here when—"

"Save it," said Whack-It, gently pushing my head down and then into the car. The leather seat squeaked as I slid across. The door slammed shut. This definitely wasn't a dream.

Whack-It walked away and pulled out his cell phone. I watched him speak to who I figured had to be one of my parents. Fucking A. Feelings of guilt swam through my veins and punched my chest despite the fact I had nothing to do with this fire. I was accused. I was a suspect sitting in the backseat of a cop car. The obvious assumption was I had started it. It was all adding up and a visceral feeling like I actually *had* done it unfurled within me.

No. I'm innocent here.

"Hey!" I screamed. "Let me outta here! I didn't do anything wrong! I was trying to help!"

Whack-It turned and gave me a passing glance like I was nothing more than a beggar on the street, and with as much disdain. He pressed a button on his phone as Mrs. Tomlinson emerged from the house, leaning on Fireman One for support. They shambled toward the ambulance.

Okay, I won't be in here long. The Tomlinsons will tell them what happened and it will clear my name.

Clear my name. *God! Do you hear yourself? You're a criminal. And you'll always be a criminal in this town.*

The irony of this whole situation dawned on me as, through the window, I spotted both my parents rushing past the cop car to meet Officer Tackett. He gave a nod in my direction and Mom shot me a look like a laser beam and I had to look away. *Of course they all think you did it. You're Firebug. So don't look away. Look them in the eye.*

I tried listening to what they were saying to each other, but they were too quiet and I was encased in metal and glass. Then Dad's voice rose up and cut through it all: "Let me speak to my son, Arnie."

There was reluctance in Whack-It's response. Maybe he was just doing his job or maybe he was imagining himself in a TV cop drama and was playing out how his character should react. He shifted his weight from one hip to the other, gave a thousand-yard-stare at my father and nodded once.

The car door opened, and Dad leaned in.

"The truth, Daniel," he said. "Did you do this?"

"No!" I shouted. "I saw the broken window and I went to help."

He studied me long enough to determine if I was lying or not, a study I'd been the subject of more times than I can count. He was far too familiar with all my "tells" to misread my guilt if there was any admission of it. A parent knows their child.

"Take those cuffs off my son, Arnie."

"With all due respect, Ben, it's far too coincidental that

your son just happened to be here at a scene where arson could be involved—"

"It wasn't arson, Whack-It!" I yelled venomously.

Quick reprimand from my father: "Watch it, Daniel."

Tackett ignored my outburst. "We need to question Glen and Edie before I feel comfortable releasing him."

"So go question Glen and Edie," Dad said, "but take those cuffs off my boy first."

"You're not telling me how to do my job, are ya, Ben?"

Dad might have cracked a smile at that but remained stoic and respectful. "Of course not. I'm asking you, father to father, to not treat my boy like a criminal until you have reason to. He's not going anywhere, Arnie. Please take the cuffs off."

The muscles in Whack-It's jaw tightened and two jets of steam shot out of his nose like a dragon. He took the key from his pocket and with a curt nod, ordered me to lean forward. A few clicks later, my wrists were freed but the sting remained.

Dad smiled politely. "Thank you, Arnie."

Whack-It said nothing in reply and quickly moved to the ambulance where the Tomlinsons were being examined. Mom leaned in to look me over, and despite my innocence, I could practically read her mind: *What have you gotten yourself into this time?*

"Okay," she said. "Start talking."

I gave my statement that night about four or five times to my parents, the paramedics, ol' Whack-It, and whoever else on the scene felt like they needed an explanation. Being that I was the only one with visual acuity greater than 20/60 to have seen the creature from Elsewhere, its involvement in this fiasco remained undiscovered. Mr. Tomlinson had his own interpretation:

"It was a damned coyote, damned *big* one, jumped right through m' front winda, can you believe it? Goddamned thing, I'd 'a put a bullet in 'im if I'd had m' rifle. Someone call Henry, tell 'im there's a goddamned coyote on the loose."

My version of events essentially corroborated Mr. and Mrs. Tomlinson's—an "animal" had attacked Mr. Tomlinson, the faulty lights on the downed Christmas tree had started the fire, and I'd happened along to investigate ("And THANK GAWD," Mrs. Tomlinson had said. "He more than likely saved our lives!"). So, by the end of it I was far from being the suspect. I was the freakin' hero. I particularly loved that part, loved seeing the forehead wrinkles smooth out on my parents, seeing an almost (dare I say it?) *proud* look in their eyes! See? Your son's not a *complete* fuck-up. The truth was I didn't do much to save anyone; Mr. Tomlinson had been the one to call 911 and the "coyote" had taken off all on its own. But hey, this was a rare occurrence, me being the *good* guy and it felt kinda nice, so I happily accepted some credit for saving the day. Especially after my near incarceration for arson.

The ambulance took the Tomlinsons to the hospital for further care, and Mom, Dad and I walked home in a fall of tiny snowflakes.

"That's just so bizarre," Mom started. She turned to Dad. "Honey, are coyotes usually that aggressive, that...bold?"

I spoke before Dad could answer. "It wasn't a coyote." Then, "Did you find Chloe?"

Dad shook his head solemnly. "No."

Mom touched my shoulder. "What do you mean it wasn't a coyote?"

"It wasn't a coyote. I don't know what it was, but it wasn't a coyote."

"But Mr. Tomlinson said—"

"Mr. Tomlinson is legally blind."

God, could I have used a drink right about then. Beer, whiskey, a fucking wine cooler, anything. I think my colleagues at AA would grant me this one reprieve. If they'd just borne witness to a being from another dimension, and then been cuffed and thrown into a cop car for a crime they didn't commit, I'd grant one for *them*. Hell, I'd be the designated driver on a Daniel-sponsored bar hop.

I could feel my nerves going and the only thing I knew that would settle them was a drink. But I'd have to deal.

"What did it look like, Daniel? The coyote-that-wasn't-a-coyote," Mom asked.

A demon. A ghost. Something out of a Guillermo del Toro movie. An Edvard Munch painting.

"*The Scream*," I said in a weak voice.

Mom's face looked like she'd just bitten into a lemon. "Huh?"

The snow continued to fall, the flakes increasing in size. An icy breeze picked up and swooped down the nape of my neck. A violent tremor racked me.

"I don't know. I guess it was a coyote."

"Daniel, are you all right?" Mom put her hand on my shoulder again, this time gripping it.

Dumb question, Mom. Of course I'm not! I just had a Close Encounter of the Third Kind before getting tossed into a cop car like some thieving hooligan!

"Fine, just a little...you know...in shock."

I looked over at Dad. He'd been watching me this whole

time. I could feel his eyes on me, as if waiting for the moment when I'd finally look at him, and when I did, he told me everything I needed without uttering a single word.

I know it wasn't a coyote.

The Lone Bellow *front man Zach Williams credits the band's success…*The Lone Bellow *front man Zach Williams credits the band's success…*The Lone Bellow *front man Zach Williams credits…*

Like an errant groove in a record causes it to skip, the experience at the Tomlinson's kept me from completing the sentence in the *Rolling Stone* article. My mind was racing in too many directions, distracted by too many questions for it to focus. I'd thought the best thing for me to do (since drinking ten or fifteen beers wasn't an option) was to relax in my bed, read a magazine until sleep overtook me, and wake the following morning with a fresh head and calmed nerves. Laying there, magazine in hand, my eyes glazing the words but failing to absorb them, proved my little strategy was not going to work. The Lone Bellow *front man Zach Williams* (that face…that face, *The Scream*) *credits the band's success* (impossible…and it's out there…and it saw me…it saw me…what is it? Where did it come from? My god where did it come from?) *credits the band's success—*

A knock on my door took the needle off the record.

"Come in."

The door swung in, Dad's hand on the knob. He had the look of a man who was in desperate need of sleep, and I wondered what the heck he'd been doing all day.

"How ya doing?" he asked.

I shrugged with a grin. "All right."

Dad stepped into my room and quietly shut the door behind him. From that simple action I got the distinct feeling we were about to broach something big, obviously something private. I set the magazine down and sat up. Dad paused, his hand still on the doorknob as if second-guessing the need to close it. Or maybe second-guessing having the conversation we were about to have.

Chloe's dead. He lied before and now he's going to tell me the truth. He found her and she's dead.

Dad took a seat at the foot of my bed and stared hard at me with his sharp blue eyes.

"I want to know what you really saw tonight."

I stared back at him silently. His words hung in the air like a bad smell. The last thing I wanted to do was talk about the *it* (that face *that face*) and relive an experience I had barely begun to process. But at the same time, the look Dad was giving me felt like we had a shared secret and both of us knew it.

I took a deep breath and told him exactly what I'd seen. Throughout, he never frowned and never looked at me like I was crazy and making stuff up. In fact, his face hardly moved. And when I finished, all he did was take a deep breath and let it out slowly. He cast his eyes down at the floor and bit at the tip of a fingernail. I could almost see his mind working through the layers of skin, bone, and blood. Something was about to come out, for good or ill.

His gaze returned to me.

"I don't want to talk about this yet with your mother and sister. I told Soren the same thing. Are we clear?"

I nodded.

Dad cleared his throat.

"Henry showed me something today while we were

looking for Chloe. Out at the Wickstrom ranch. He'd gotten a call from Bert to hurry over, and once he saw it...he radioed me..."

Dad and Soren had started locally: cruising slowly up and down nearby neighborhoods calling Chloe's name, checking in with neighbors here and there to see if they'd spotted a large German Shepherd roaming about. Henry, Ferdinand's leading (and only) name in Animal Control, was also on the alert, patrolling not only for a runaway dog, but also a predator posing a threat to pets across town. Dad had told him about the mutilated animal carcass he'd found in the culvert, told him in great detail the state of the animal and to be on the alert for a roving coyote, wolf, or a wildcat. Henry said he'd gotten one similar report two days ago, a pregnant horse gutted, the fetus missing, presumably devoured. He'd never seen anything like it. Never heard of anything like that happening. "But sure as shit that mare was hollowed out like a Halloween punkin," Henry had told my father. "No foal, no nothin'."

Henry's voice had later blared across Dad's CB sounding like he was trying his best to keep from panicking. Shaky and low, Henry had said Dad's name just as Soren had gotten back in the truck from taking a leak on the side of a dirt road.

"Henry, come back..."

"Benny...you still out on the Camas Road?" Quick scratch of CB static.

"No, we circled back at Stillwater. Where are you? Any luck?"

"I'm out at the Wickstrom Ranch. Got a call from Bert 'bout twenty minutes ago." Static scratch.

"Henry, any sign of Chloe?"

"Sorry, Ben, no. But…" Static scratch.

"Everything all right Henry?"

Silence.

Silence.

"Henry?"

"Ben…you might wanna come out here…"

"Why? What did you find?"

"Just come out…but you leave your boy in the truck, you hear me?"

Dad parked behind Henry's Toyota 4-Runner with the "Animal Control" sign on the driver's side door. He spotted Henry running across Bert's pasture to meet him.

"You stay here, Soren, I won't be long."

"But Dad—"

"Son, I'll only tell you once."

Soren, ever the petulant one, sighed loud enough to fog a spot on the windshield and turned his head to look away from Dad.

Grabbing his sunglasses, Dad exited the vehicle.

Henry kicked up skiffs of snow as he stomped out of the field. Dad slid his sunglasses on and waited patiently beside his pick-up. A growing sense of dread filled his guts. Whatever Henry was about to show him would more than likely stick to his memory and steal his sleep tonight. He was not typically faint of heart, but he'd never heard fear in Henry's voice quite like he had today on the CB. Henry was a solid, rational, meat-and-potatoes kind of man. Whatever had shaken him had to be nightmare-worthy.

The sun glared blindingly off the white field.

Henry, huffing out great clouds, finally reached the pick-up.

"What's going on, Henry?"

Henry's cheeks were red apples. The little bit of hair that poked out from beneath his black cotton beanie was wet and clumped with sweat.

"Follow me. Behind the barn."

"You remember that mare I told you about?" said Henry.

The snow was deep and the trudging was slow. The barn was still several yards away. Dad scanned the field for Bert's cattle and found them, all in a tight cluster, on the opposite side of the field. They looked like a family of hamsters at this distance, small and huddled on top of one another. If the fence hadn't been there to keep them in, he doubted they'd still be here at all.

"Yeah, you said she'd been hollowed out?"

"That's right."

They passed the barn and an old horse trailer that looked like it hadn't been used in years. It sat in the fresh white snow with rusty hinges and a few bullet-holes, looking more like trash Bert had yet to dispose of than a working trailer.

Half a football field-length away the snow was no longer white.

Dad stopped. Breath caught in his lungs. It didn't look real; didn't seem it could possibly *be* real. More like the setup for a horror movie film shoot. But this was no set. That wasn't gallons of fake blood splashed gratuitously over the white ground for mere effect. The large bovine bodies weren't models or puppets or actors in suits. The horror was real. There really *was* that much blood, impossible as it may seem.

Dad slowly removed his sunglasses.

"Three springers. All of 'em set to calve in three t' four months," said Henry. "All three dead. Gutted. Just like the mare."

Dad realized his mouth was hanging open and closed it. A wave of nausea broke on the banks of his innards, and he had to draw a deep, icy breath through his nostrils. He exhaled smoothly.

"A real horror show, ain't it?" said Henry, continuing on across the field to where Bert Wickstrom stood, the old cowboy baffled and brokenhearted.

Dad's first step landed on a few pink spots in the snow. His next step crunched upon pink snow with a few red spots. And then there was only red.

"Howdy, Ben," said Bert as Dad finally caught up to the other two men. Bert stood over one of the dead cows, shaking his head as if to say *Well ain't that the darndest thing…*

"Afternoon, Bert."

Bert looked like a typical cowboy: dusty Stetson shielding a sunbaked face slashed with deep wrinkles, thick sideburns, lower lip bulging with a plug of tobacco, tight Wranglers, brown leather coat with a white wool lining. He'd give you the shirt off his back if you needed it. Generous and kind beyond measure, the man had only two noticeable flaws: the index finger on his right hand was missing on account of a combine harvester incident, and he liked to take to the bottle. He was a fellow AA compatriot and always had a warm smile for me, brown with tobacco but always free of judgment.

"Helluva sight, eh?" said Bert, his voice low and scratchy. He spat a stream of tobacco juice on the red ground.

"So. What are we thinkin' here?" asked Dad, staring down at the massacred carcass.

"Well," started Bert, looking over his shoulder at the other two slaughtered animals. A pair of crows were already picking at the carrion. "Three cows—pregnant—all of 'em opened up and emptied out. No sign o' th' calves."

Dad searched the ground surrounding the dead cow. "Any tracks?"

"None," said Bert. "Damnedest thing. But I know whatever done this didn't *fly* in."

"Look at the flesh, Ben, there at the opening. The edges," said Henry.

Dad knelt for a closer look at the carcass. He grimaced involuntarily. The crows behind him squawked and cawed.

The cow had been ripped open from udder to brisket, presumably by a claw or talon given the ragged, unclean incision. Entrails, already frozen, spilled out onto the crimson snow. The loose flaps of flesh where the belly had been separated were blackened at the edges, as if they'd been burned, cauterized. Dad imagined a red-hot poker doing the job, slicing the cow wide open like unzipping a brown leather jacket. But what sense did that make? He reached out with a tentative finger to touch the blackened flesh only to find it didn't *feel* charred. It was sticky—

"Holy shit!"

The three men whirled around to find Soren standing just outside the massacre.

"Damn it Soren, what did I tell you?" snapped Dad, standing upright.

"Come on Dad, I couldn't miss *this*!"

"Go back to the truck."

"But I've already seen it!"

"Soren, go."

"So much blood…"

"Guess what, now you're grounded."

"Dad, it's Christmas!"

"Keep arguing Soren, I dare ya."

Soren closed his mouth, but his eyes glared back.

Dad turned to Bert.

"The other two…they look just like this one?"

Bert nodded and spit. "A-yup."

"And no prints?"

"Not a one."

Dad crunched through the snow toward the other dead cows. Bert and Henry followed. Soren hesitated, his eyes combing over the grotesque display of blood and guts and ripped flesh. When it seemed he wouldn't be told to return to the truck again, he tromped after the men.

"What kinda animal guts a springer, takes the calf, and doesn't leave a single track?" asked Henry.

"What kind of animal does it three times in one night?" said Dad.

The second cow was a repeat of the first: hollowed out, torn flesh edged in black.

"Ain't no animal leaves a black residue behind like that," said Bert. "None that I know of."

Dad shook his head. "No."

"Could it be a person did this?" asked Henry.

"It'd take a pickup to haul out three calves. Weren't no tire tracks nor boot tracks," said Bert.

"Chupacabra," said Soren. "I saw a show once on the History Channel, looked a lot like this."

The crows continued to cackle at each other and were joined by two more. They pecked and pulled at the sinew like red chewing gum.

Dad sighed, his brow furrowed.

"Three missing calves, one foal, one fawn. All taken in utero."

"Fawn?" I said, raising an eyebrow.

Dad took a breath, stretched his lips across his teeth.

"In the culvert. By the level of development, it clearly hadn't been born yet. I didn't want to upset you."

"Dad, I'm nineteen."

"It wasn't something I felt you needed to know or see, son. Period."

Something struck me.

"Dad, that explains why it didn't get Mr. and Mrs. Tomlinson. They're too old, this thing wants babies!"

Dad hushed me. "Keep your voice down."

"Why? I think Mom and Lilly should know what's out there! I think—"

"I don't want to jump to any conclusions yet, Daniel."

"Dad, this *thing* has been to our house—go look at the garage door, there are black *claw* marks there just like the sticky stuff you described on the dead cows!"

"It's just going to needlessly alarm your mother—"

"Needlessly?"

"We don't even know what—*it*—is, Dan, or what it wants—"

"I think it's pretty clear what it wants—"

"Which is why I don't want your mother to worry."

"But she's not a baby, and neither is Lilly."

"Son, drop it please, I'm not telling your mother. We don't know enough about what is going on here—"

"Why would Mom worry?"

"Daniel…"

"Benjamin…"

"Because your mom is pregnant."

I took a breath to speak but my words were lost and suddenly I had nothing to replace them with. My jaw just hung slack.

Pregnant.

"We were going to surprise you kids on Christmas morning with the news," said Dad, rubbing the side of his face. His scruff scratched against his calloused hand. "So, you get it now? I don't want her jumping to conclusions. Shit, *I* don't want to jump to conclusions. So please keep your mouth shut, Dan."

"How long have you known?"

"Not long. A few weeks. Your mother is calling it an 'Oopsie'."

"Oopsie?"

"Unintended."

I snickered.

"For now, this is between you and me, Dan. Soren, the little shit, knows about the cows. But everything else we discussed stays here, understood? It does not leave this room."

I nodded. "Yeah, okay."

"Alright then."

Dad stood. In a gesture he hadn't done since I was a small boy, he kissed the top of my head and ruffled my hair.

"I have a feeling Chloe is still out there. We're gonna find her, son."

I gave a half-hearted smile.

"We'll talk more in the morning. Get some sleep."

Dad left the room, closing the door behind him.

CHAPTER FOUR

When I was a kid I liked to pretend that our house was haunted (I would years later play a different version of the same game with my buddies inside a farmer's "abandoned" country house before razing it to the ground). The floorboards upstairs would naturally creak and pop as the house heated beneath a summertime sun, and I would tell the babysitter it was ghosts. She would give me a look like *Not this again*, and I'd grab her hand and drag her upstairs to investigate. She usually played along up until the point where she'd actually get spooked (which always gave me a warm thrill!) and then turn me outside to play in the street like a normal kid.

Sometimes I would spin yarns about the people who died in the house and the tormented spirits they left behind. "He was an old farmer named McDonald…" (at age seven I was already employing the cardinal rule of writers everywhere— write what you know—but could turn it dark on a dime)— "and he died of a zillion spider bites!" (Babysitter: "Where the hell-I-mean-*heck* do you come up with this stuff, Daniel?"). I'd walk stealthily through the house, my ears pricked, waiting for another groan from expanding floorboards, a snap from walls as they stretched, or some other physical sign there was an entity roaming the bedrooms or hallways. I would rip back the shower curtain expecting to find the ghoulish McDonald or some other spirit and breathe a dramatic sigh of relief when the basin appeared ghost-free (I'd obviously seen something similar in some movie I wasn't supposed to have seen. Odds are Dad was to blame).

Our laundry room was in the basement, along with the water heater, which lived behind a neat little hinged panel disguised to look like part of the wall. It was too small for any adult but the perfect size for a child. Before Soren and Lilly were old enough and it became prime hide-and-seek real estate, I imagined that behind that little door lay the portal through which the ghosts could pass from their world into ours. Whenever I found it left slightly ajar, I would bolt over and slam it shut. Then, my pulse quickening, I would turn my head and look over my shoulder (very slowly, of course, for dramatic effect, like they did in the movies). *Who knows what has escaped into our world*, I would think, and my daily mission would begin.

I only ever spooked myself once. It was nighttime and Mom and Dad had been fighting. From my bedroom I could hear the whole thing:

Mom: "I can't remember the last time you actually paid me a compliment."

Dad: "Are you serious? Does your ego need my approval so much that you're seriously bitching about a lack of compliments? You know I love you and that should be enough."

Mom: "Well it's not enough, Benjamin, okay, it's not. I need to hear you *verbally* express it, you know that; we've been through this time and time again and you still don't get it. It feels like you know what I need and purposefully withhold it because it's not your style or something."

Dad: "I just don't see the point in saying things over and over again, Renee, when you already know them!"

Mom: "Because it makes me happy! I do things for you all the time just because I know it makes *you* happy!"

It went on like that for another twenty-five minutes or so before they gave it up and went to bed. That argument scared me far more than any of my made-up ghosts ever had.

I lay in bed wide-awake, my anxiety from the argument rendering me sleepless. My bedroom door always started out closed when I went to bed but was now fully opened; it was something I always insisted upon, and Mom would lovingly oblige every night before she went to bed. I liked to have a clear view into Mom and Dad's room if I were to wake in the middle of the night. It always made me feel better. I was somehow less alone that way, I guess.

Through the darkness, I saw a shade, darker than the surrounding darkness, glide gracefully across the wall like a shadow. My breath caught in my throat. I blinked. I rewound the scene in my head and watched it on instant replay. Something was out there. I could've stayed safely in bed but was overcome with the need to act. What if the portal had been left open? Ghosts in the daylight were different than ghosts at night. In the daylight they could be easily dealt with. At night, they were stronger. Meaner. And actually scary. I supposed I could wait and deal with them tomorrow, but the likelihood of dozens crossing over under the cloak of night was almost guaranteed, and I just couldn't sleep knowing these things were possibly in my room, staring at me, their ghastly, translucent faces waiting for me to open my eyes so they could scream at me.

I got out of bed and crept to the basement, the hairs on the back of my neck standing at full attention. I remember feeling proud of myself that I'd braved the darkness without having to flick on a single light. I didn't want Mom or Dad to suddenly wake and find a light on and start asking questions. This was my fight. And only I could end it.

I found the neat little door cracked open about an inch, and a red glow coming from behind it.

My first thought was *I did this, I created this, my imagination is so strong it brought the portal to life and now ghosts are real and now I'm scared for real and wish I'd never played this game and gotten out of bed and I want my Mom.* I let out a breath, took another one, a shallow one, and held it. I stared at the glowing red portal. It stared back. And for a moment I was sure I'd soon be surrounded by a wicked horde of luminous ghosts like something out of one of those scary movies Dad watched. They'd be angry because they were dead and thirsty for the taste of my fear and they'd scream and moan and repeat my name in low, horrible voices: *Dannniel, Dannnnniel.* So why wasn't I running back to my room, back to the safety of my bed where my blanket/shield waited to hide me from evil?

My heart punched against my ribcage, drummed in my ears. I took a step toward the portal. My imagination spun like someone flipping rapidly through television channels. What was I going to see on the other side of that door? What hellish energy was the source of that fiery red glow? Would boney hands dripping with decaying flesh suddenly reach out and pull me inside? Anything was possible now that *this* was possible. And I had created it. Despite my fear my feet brought me closer to the portal without hesitation. I could hear the low hum of the water heater, something I'd heard dozens of times before, but now it was the drone of the opened Hellgate.

Suddenly, I didn't want to see. Icy, white fear seized my nerves and I didn't want to look inside. I didn't want to know. What if whatever I saw literally scared me to death? What if whatever horror lay within gave me nightmares that would plague me well into my adult years? It was something a seven-year-old couldn't quite comprehend, but it compelled me to lurch forward and slam the door shut like I was swatting at a fly.

I stood there for a full minute in the darkness catching my breath. Behind the door, the water heater continued to purr. And then, like water down a drain, my fear emptied my body. A semblance of rationality returned, and the thought that the shadow I'd seen upstairs could have been created by a passing car, a tree branch, or simply just a trick of the light seemed far more possible. I took a breath and opened the portal.

The evil red light still shone brightly but now I glimpsed the source. It was a very small square on the cylindrical heater and reminded me of the taillights on Mom's car, and its only purpose, it seemed, was to indicate that the water heater was on. I stared at it as whatever remained of my fear dissolved, and then shut the door. There was no sigh of relief, no self-aware grin of embarrassment, just the small click of the door latching as it closed and my desire to return immediately to my bedroom.

So why was I terrified to turn around?

I stood stock-still, my skin slowly prickling.

Turn around, it's not real, there's no such thing as ghosts, while simultaneously, *That's what they want you to believe and as soon as you turn around there'll be bony faces with empty sockets and moldering flesh and mouths stretched impossibly wide so they can fit you in.*

I tugged at the elastic waistband of my pajama bottoms. I bit nervously on my lower lip. My breaths came in short, quick inhalations and exhalations.

I was preparing.

You can't just stand here all night, and no sooner had that thought taunted me than the urge to pee flicked at my tiny seven-year-old wiener. It wasn't a weight in my bladder that had gradually increased with a slow sense of urgency, but a quick spark, a bright shock that streaked down to the tip of my penis. Fear pee. The worst. I had to turn around within the next sixty seconds or else explain my urine-soaked PJs and the wet spot on the floor in the morning.

It's not real, it's just the water heater, there's no such thing as ghosts...

I thought of the relief I'd feel once back in bed, that warm, safe feeling of being back where I belonged, nestled in with the covers up around my chin and my stuffed turtle held tightly to my chest. I wanted it. I wanted it now. Just one obstacle. One terrifying obstacle that if I overcame, I'd never be afraid of anything again. I could brave the worst from here on out.

Turn around.

I can't.

You have to.

They'll be there.

They're not real. You made them up.

I don't want to see.

You're gonna pee your pants.
So I'll pee my pants. Not the first time.
Go to bed. It'll feel so nice.
It will.
You should've just turned on a light, then it wouldn't be as scary.
You're right.
Turn around, Daniel.

So I did. I took a breath, remembered that time last summer when I was scared to death to jump off the diving board at swimming lessons but did it. All the kids in the pool cheering me on...my tiny shivering body alone there on that bouncy plank of aircraft-grade aluminum...and I did it. I just plugged my nose, hoped I wouldn't drown, and jumped.

I hadn't drowned, and I had felt like a warrior hero afterward.

I must've had a crazed look of defiance on my face because after I turned and found no leering shrouded skulls, I felt my face relax; my lips smoothed out of their sneer, my eyes stopped bulging, and my flaring dragon nostrils returned to normal size. What had I been trying to do? Scare the ghosts? Make myself bigger and scarier to intimidate them? *Them*? My shoulders sank, my buttocks unclenched, and my breath left my lungs in a long, shaky hiss through my teeth, wriggling the loose one in the front. The fear pee hadn't subsided yet so my first stop on my way back to bed would be the toilet. But the toilet upstairs, not the one down here. I didn't want to spend another second down here alone.

After that night, I stopped pretending our house was haunted. I don't know if it was the evil red glow, the fear of thinking I'd brought to life my own nightmarish games, or Mom and Dad's disturbing argument, but after that night, ghosts in my house didn't much appeal to me. So, many years later, the ghosts took up residence in the abandoned house that belonged to the farmer. Deep down I still wanted to believe that such things could exist...just not within the comforting confines of my home.

And now, after recounting that childhood memory, I shook my head in derision at the ignorance of that little boy. And that fifteen-year-old, too. I *wanted* to believe, but never really did. Not truly. And now that I know for a fact—beyond the shadow of a doubt, really—that there *are* things that go bump in the night and there *are* supernatural creatures lurking in dark places and there *are* horrible, unexplainable things that defy logic, science, and scripture...

I had been *right* to be scared to turn around.

CHAPTER FIVE

I love my mother, I really do. I've always seen her as the most rational one in the family, the pillar, the rock. Stubborn as all hell, but usually correct in her thinking. She's always the first one to come to my defense when I fuck up, even as she's plotting my punishment. She's tender and loving and she makes me laugh. She gives the best hugs. She's thoughtful in ways I've come to take for granted, but that never seems to upset her. She's nearly unflappable and frighteningly intelligent and a woman other women aspire to be.

I love my mother. But when she told me she'd pimped me out to some folks in the Raddock Addition, I hated her fucking guts.

The conversation went something like this:

"So, I got you a few more gigs."

"Gigs?"

"Yeah, you're gonna be shoveling the Blankenships', the Bells', and the Greens' up in the Raddock Addition. They're very grateful."

"*What?*"

"I didn't stutter and my volume was sufficient, you heard me."

"That is such bullshit!"

"Language, Daniel…"

"What the crap, Mom, what do you think I am, your little slave?"

"No, you're my son."

"You're like…pimping me out, like I'm some kind of prostitute!"

"I like to think of myself more as an agent who's getting you gigs."

"Stop calling them *gigs*, they're not *gigs*!"

"The Greens are expecting you in about an hour."

"Fuck that!"

"Daniel, what do you think this is, your Christmas vacation? You're on holiday? No school, no job, no responsibilities? You sir, are on life probation. In case you've forgotten, let me remind you that you nearly flunked out of your first semester of college because you decided drinking alcohol was a better use of your time than studying."

"Mom—"

"You wasted mine and your father's money. You wasted *your* time. But the worst part is you wasted your potential. And talent. And that is something, in time, you will learn to regret the most."

"So shoveling neighbors driveways and sidewalks is somehow a good use of my potential?"

"Of course not, no, it's punishment. Duh."

"This is unbelievable. I'm nineteen years old."

"Wake up, Daniel. Take your licks. Own them. Learn from them. Move forward."

"Do you know how embarrassing it is being the neighborhood shovel boy?"

"This is where I say something like, 'You should have thought about that before you made your rotten choices' or something, right? Greens' in an hour, Blankenships' right after, and dress warmly, it's supposed to dip into the teens today."

"Can I at least drive my car up there?"

"Um, car privileges revoked, remember?"

"But it's fucking freezing!"

"Say the F-word again, Daniel, I dare you."

"This is inhumane. What you are doing is inhumane."

"You should call CPS, though I hardly think they'd consider you a child anymore. You're nineteen, after all."

I left the conversation and went to my room, grabbed my North Face jacket, gloves, and blue-and-gray striped beanie. When I returned to the kitchen, Mom raised one eyebrow.

"The Greens aren't expecting you for an hour, Dan."

"Well maybe I'll surprise them with my real go-get-'er attitude."

She smiled sarcastically.

I glared.

The little shit in me was bound and determined to have the last word. As I pulled on my jacket and hat, I thought of my parting sentiment.

"Congratulations, by the way."

"For what?"

"Your 'Oopsie.'"

I walked out the door without Mom getting in another word.

I win.

The Greens were the wealthiest family in Ferdinand. A byproduct of this wealth was an opulent three-story home complete with a four-car garage and crescent-shaped driveway that took up at least half an acre. I took one look at the accumulated foot of snow on that horseshoe driveway and seriously considered going on the lam.

"Bullshit," I sighed, leaning on the handle of my snow shovel. "So fucked up."

Then I suddenly remembered Mr. and Mrs. Tomlinson and realized things could be worse. I stabbed the shovel blade into the white powder and it scraped against the cement driveway. The sound broke the eerie winter silence.

I got to work.

During the course of the two-plus hours it took me to clear the Greens' driveway, my thoughts ran the gamut:

Chloe.

Where is she?

Is she dead?

Did it get her?

I could use a beer.

No, a Whiskey Seven.

I'm horny.

Super horny.

I need to pick up my guitar again.

Fuck, its cold.

This is horseshit.

Mom's a bitch.

It's been too long since I've written any new music.

I really want that Whiskey Seven.

I wonder how the old crew from high school is doing.

I wonder if any of them know I'm back.

I wonder if any of them know why.

Firebug.

Fuck that name.

That thing, that alien, *what is it, where did it come from?*

Why babies, why fetuses? Why fire?

Lilly is gonna die if Chloe doesn't come back.

I wonder if Mom and Dad got me anything for Christmas?

I've been pretty naughty this year. Santa would have crossed me off his list.

I'd like to have as much money as the Greens.

Mrs. Green is a doctor, Mr. Green is an ex-military general-turned-lawyer, retired.

I don't want to be either of those.

I wonder when I'm gonna get my car back.

I miss my car.

I'm super, super horny.

I didn't notice when it started to snow but once I finally did, I felt like Sisyphus endlessly and fruitlessly pushing that boulder up the hill only to watch it roll back down.

The Greens', the Blankenships', and the Bells' took me four hours combined. It was dark by the time my work was done.

The cold had worked its way underneath my jacket, and as I trudged home, my mind filled with warmer thoughts: clear skies, green fields of sweet clover, hot breezes preempting a summer thunderstorm, floating lazily down the river on a black tube and burning that tender flesh inside your arms, going barefoot, wearing tank-tops every single day, the beautiful, bronzed skin of a pretty girl...

"Dan?"

Immediately I cringed. It was a young female's voice, a

young female who saw me walking down the middle of the street with a snow shovel. If my face wasn't red from the cold already, it certainly flushed now.

I turned to see whom the voice belonged to.

At first, I couldn't tell. She was backlit from the yellow porch-light glow, just a silhouette, and wearing a bulky Patagonia jacket. The way the light shot through her messy auburn shoulder-length hair made it look like fire. That hair gave her away.

It was Rebecca Bailey, my high school crush, numero uno deposit in the Spank Bank. I'd last seen her very briefly at Lilly's Christmas pageant. She'd waved. I'd waved back. Then she'd left with her boyfriend. I'd completely forgotten she lived in the Raddock Addition.

"Oh. Hey," I said, sending her a half-hearted wave. She wriggled her fingers in response.

"I thought that was you. Whatcha doin'?" she asked, her breath a bright white vapor. "Come over here."

"Nah, I got to get on home," is what I wanted to say. "I don't really want to get into a conversation with you because how I became a giant loser shoveling driveways this winter is bound to come up and it's going to lessen the possibility that you're going to have sex with me, never mind that you have a boyfriend or husband or whatever he is and that you're pregnant. It will come down to me being a college burnout with no job and no future and an alcohol problem and a fondness for setting things on fire and then I'm probably going to mention that *thing*, that *it* because it's almost all I can think about lately because it scares the shit out of me and then you'll have one more reason to not have sex with me: you'll think I'm crazy. So no, I'm not gonna come over there. I'm gonna get on home like a good boy or else my mommy will find even more driveways for me to shovel."

But instead, I crossed the street and crunched up the snowy walkway to her porch.

"Want me to shovel this? I came prepared."

She laughed, a real laugh, one from the belly, not just one to make me feel good. That made me smile.

"No, that's quite all right," she said.

I got closer and her features came into view. I always thought she was a peculiar mix of that chick who plays Hermione in *Harry Potter* and Katy Perry. After a semester post-high school, I found her slanted more towards Katy, and I liked it. Her cheeks were high but not sharp, and rosy from the cold. Her mouth was like a gracefully cresting wave, lips curling at the ends and rising in the middle. Those eyes, big and bright, and that hair...a beautiful, flaming, cascading girly mess. All that was the same as it was before, but now more... woman. A semester at college looked good on her.

"Sorry I didn't come over and talk to you the other night," she said. "I had to pee so bad, and Brett wanted to go home, like, immediately so I just kinda beelined it."

"Oh, no worries," I said. "I get it."

"You do? You pregnant too? 'Cause I'd love to commiserate about how running to the bathroom every twenty minutes has become the norm." She rubbed her belly on top of the puffy Patagonia. It made a quiet *shushing* sound, friction against nylon. I loved that she used the words *commiserate* and *norm*.

"No, not pregnant but I keep trying!" I said, and then realized that joke would be funnier if I was gay. Fuck. Oh well. She laughed anyway. "What are you doing out here, its freezing."

"Is it? It feels good to me, that house was roasting. And I love watching the snow fall."

"Yeah," was all I could manage to reply with. I looked up at the sky and pretended to also love watching the snowfall.

"So, no offense but I heard you, like, got kicked out of school or something?"

"I did not get kicked out," I said, and, from the startled look on her face, with perhaps a touch too much venom. She looked embarrassed. Fuck again. "My folks pulled me out," I clarified, "which...doesn't sound any better, does it?" I grinned self-consciously.

She grinned too. "No, not really. I'm sorry for—"

"No, don't be, its just—"

"Dan, it's none of my business, seriously—"

"—been a long day and—"

"Well, do you wanna come in? Mom and Dad are gone for the night, so I invited a few people over for a bonfire in the backyard."

"Um..."

Remember: house arrest. Mom. Punishment. Strict orders.

Rebecca watched me battling my indecision. "The boys are drinking some beers, I'm sure they'd share..."

House arrest. Mom. Punishment.

But also: *Mom. Bitch.*

"Yeah, I can stay for a beer or two."

Rebecca smiled. "Good!"

She turned and that lovely mess of auburn hair fanned out like a twirling dress, and I could smell the shampoo she used. Her bright white breath swept across her right cheek as she opened the front door. I left my shovel propped against the porch railing.

Cinnamon and pine and Adele's latest album greeted me as we walked across the threshold. The living room was modest and clean and brightly lit with Christmas décor and the almost-too-tall-for-the-ceiling Christmas tree. Compared to outside the house *was* roasting, but it felt good, and I was relieved to be out of the cold.

"I can take your jacket and stuff," said Rebecca, unzipping her own. I stripped off my winter gear and handed it to her. She tossed it all on the back of a chair. I giggled.

"I could have done that myself," I said.

"But what kind of hostess would I be?" She grinned.

Was she being...*flirty*? Suddenly my heartbeat took it up a notch.

In the kitchen, the sliding-glass door to the backyard opened. The man standing behind it crushed out the butt of a cigarette on the sole of his boot and entered the house.

"Oh babe, come here, I want you to meet my friend from high school," said Rebecca enthusiastically. The boyfriend could have made an expression, but it was undetectable beneath his full hipster beard. He complied amiably and sauntered on over.

"Dan, this is my boyfriend and baby-daddy, Brett."

Brett stuck his hand out and shook mine very firmly. "Pleasure," he said, his moving lips nothing more than a bristling of hair. For a split second I had intense beard envy.

"And this is Dan, my favorite buddy from Government class."

"Nice to meet you, man," I said.

Brett was somehow everything I wanted to be and everything I detested. His perfectly coifed hair blended into his magnificent beard like some Urban Outfitters model. His hipster plaid flannel was tucked into his hipster jeans with the rolled cuffs surrounding his stylish hipster boots. This guy was clearly not from Idaho, maybe some transplant college dude from New York? LA? Seattle? I'll bet he's a musician. Or a graphic designer. Or something involving *textiles*.

"We met at Western, in Psych 101. Hit it off immediately, obviously," said Rebecca, rubbing her belly once again. "He's majoring in Graphic Design."

Nailed it.

"Awesome," I said, nodding my head and wondering why I'd said *Awesome*.

"She's my starlight," said Brett without a trace of irony or sarcasm. I suppressed a laugh by pretending to sneeze.

"Whoa dude, are you ill?" said Brett, pulling Rebecca away from me. "We're trying to keep the fetus healthy."

"No, no, just something…in my nose, er…" Brett had rendered me speechless.

Rebecca shrugged his hands from her shoulders. "Babe, it's fine." She smiled that Hermione/Katy Perry smile. "He's so paranoid."

The sliding-glass door opened again. Coming in was a slightly newer version of an old friend.

My jaw dropped.

"Truffles?"

It didn't seem possible but somehow four months away at college had taken off a few pounds and stripped Truffles of his poor fashion sense. He was still beefy but less than he was at graduation, and I imagined I was seeing him at the very beginnings of a drastic weight-loss (which is rare for a college freshman—usually it works in the reverse). In walked a young man in raw denim and charcoal-grey sweater, black pea coat, and enough scruff on his face to qualify as a small beard. His hair was clipped short and tidy. He'd clearly been hanging out with Brett and a whole new crowd at Western University. Rebecca saw the *Wow* on my face and grinned proudly, obviously having had a hand in his makeover.

"Hey, Danny," said Truffles with a smile so bright it rivaled Dad's Christmas lights.

He came across the room and hugged me tightly. It felt good. Truffles and I had continued to hang out once my year-long grounding from razing the farmer's house was over, but he was the only one. Nick had found himself a girlfriend by then and was getting laid regularly, ergo, no time for his pyro buddy, and Casey found me disturbing so kept his distance. Truffles, however, remained loyal. Why, I don't know. I never thought I'd done much to keep his friendship and yet throughout our junior and senior years, we somehow grew closer as friends. Then we graduated, and I went to the University of Idaho and he went off to Western Washington. The end. But here he was now, and it was like no time had passed.

Truffles squeezed my shoulder. "Good to see you man, how are ya?"

"Good, good," I replied. "Just workin'...and..." I searched for something else to add but came up empty-handed.

"I heard what happened, buddy," said Truffles like he was offering his condolences. I bowed my head but quickly recovered from the shame. After all, this was Truffles I was talking to.

"And were you surprised?"

"Not really."

"Daniel the Fuck-up."

"Daniel the Fuck-up."

"I'm shoveling driveways, Truffles."

He took a hissing breath through clenched teeth. His expression of condolence doubled in intensity.

"I know," I said.

"Well if anyone needs a beer, it's you!"

"Amen!"

"But your parents…"

"—Don't have to know, Truffles, come on! You changed your look but you're still a goodie-goodie."

"Hey man, it's your funeral."

Brett slapped me on the back. "We got cold IPAs out in the snow, bro!"

There were two other people standing beside the fire pit that I didn't recognize at first. Their faces glowed with fire-light but were tucked beneath hoods. I prayed they were more college friends of Rebecca's and not high school peers to whom I'd undoubtedly have to explain what I'd been up to lately. As I was staring, trying to discern their faces, Truffles must have thought I was ogling the flickering flames in the pit. He leaned into my ear.

"Don't get any ideas, Danny boy," he said lowly.

I gave him a look but let it go. I guess I had that coming.

"Hey, Dan," said one of the hooded guests. I finally recognized her as a former underclassman, Ashley Something, a peon sophomore, and felt relieved. I barely knew her.

"Hey," I said.

Brett cracked open a can of IPA and handed it over. He offered his own beer forward to cheers. I obliged.

I stared at the open mouth of the can for a guilty second before bringing it to my lips. *Mom. Bitch.* The cold beer went down quickly. Never before had it tasted so good.

Brett handed Rebecca a flavored Pellegrino and Truffles a beer. We all moved closer to the fire. Ashley Something lit a joint and took a long drag.

"Well shit, everyone," started Brett with a beardy smile, "Merry Christmas."

"Merry Christmas, babe," said Rebecca, squeezing him.

"Merry Christmas," said Truffles.

"Yeah," said Ashley Something.

I hesitated, took another deep slug on my IPA. "Merry Christmas."

"Hey, look at that cat," said Ashley, followed by the staccato and dopey laugh of the longtime stoner. She pointed to a tree in the neighbor's backyard.

High in the branches were two silvery orange dots. The darkness cloaked most of the elm and the cat itself so all that was visible were the two reflective eyes.

"Here kittykittykitty," called Brett in a high voice.

"Kinda creepy," said the hooded girl who was not Ashley Something, speaking for the first time.

"Isn't that crazy? How its eyes are, like, flat?"

Brett tried again. "Here kittykittykitty."

Rebecca lightly slapped his arm. "Babe, don't, I'm allergic to cats."

"Plus you're preggers," said Truffles. "Ever heard of toxoplasmosis?"

"Toxopla-what?"

"You get it from cats. If a pregnant lady gets it, she can pass it on to the unborn baby and the baby can go blind."

"That is not true," interjected Brett with smug confidence. "I grew up around cats and have 20/20 vision."

"Fucking Google it, Brett: T-o-x-o-p-l—"

"I know how to spell, I'm not an idiot."

"So spell it."

"T-o-x-o-p-l-e-z-m—"

"Wrong."

"Fuck you, I have a smartphone, I don't need to know how to spell it."

While all this was going on, I never once took my eyes off those shiny orange discs. My heart pounded and my skin prickled with the icy fear of unfortunate comprehension:

The animal in the tree was no cat.

It didn't move. Not a twitch, not a blink.

It just stared.

"That's the problem with our generation, Brett, right there, perfect example of why everybody makes fun of Gen Z," continued Truffles. "We're far too reliant on our technology to know things *for* us so we don't ever have to learn them."

"Dude, you are a man-out-of-time, you should have been born in the fifties. This is where the world is headed. Deal."

No one else saw it, their attentions diverted to this stupid squabble. But very gracefully, far too graceful for even a cat, the eyes descended the elm. They did not momentarily vanish as a cat's would were it to climb down from its leafy perch, its eyes pointed away from the fire, but glided smoothly to the ground as if they belonged to a passenger on an escalator. They never faltered or turned away or blinked.

"I'll be sure to call and say, 'I told you so' when Skynet goes live," said Truffles, and then took a long drink.

"On what, your grandmother's rotary phone? Skynet will control every 'smart device' there is!" countered Brett.

"What's a Skynet?" asked the girl who wasn't Ashley Something.

"What's Skynet?" blasted Truffles, practically spitting out his beer. "You're kidding, right?"

The shiny orange discs floated to the ground. For a second, they did not move. Or at least, I didn't think they were moving.

"This is the dumbest conversation I've ever heard. Can we move on please?" said Rebecca.

And then I realized the discs were growing larger.

The *thing* was advancing on us.

"Everybody get inside," I said in a voice so small it was almost inaudible, even to myself. But Rebecca heard.

"What, Daniel?"

"Get inside right now."

She followed my frightened gaze.

The others followed hers.

It was a part of the darkness and then it was not. It *was* darkness.

Like a thick cloud of locusts, it swept across the neighbor's lawn and washed over the fence and into Rebecca's backyard. It moved fluidly like a dancing murmuration of birds, and with a chilling swiftness that shocked all our feet into immobility (except for Ashley Something, she did as I told and hightailed her ass inside). No one made a move and no one screamed—the effect of utter incomprehension—as the creature came to rest at the fire pit, its reflective eyes a brilliant orange. It stared at the fire, appearing to be heedless of our presence, and raised a wispy hand to the flames. And there it was again:

that captivated look in its strange hollow eyes, the look of one who is absolutely spellbound. The look in Casey's eyes at the flaming steel wool. The look so often in my own eyes.

One thing was certain: it had doubled in size since I'd seen it at the Tomlinsons'. Bert Wickstrom's cattle probably had something to do with that. It was now the size of a formidable eight-foot-tall black bear when reared up on hind legs, but no more substantiated; it still had to make contact with solid mass to keep it from vaporizing. In those jerky, twitchy movements it tapped the ground, the rocks surrounding the fire pit, a nearby bench. Through my peripheral vision I could see Brett slowly backing away, and that's when the creature finally paid us attention.

It saw me first (and oh fuck me, was that a glimmer of *recognition* in its face?) but quickly turned its disturbing, hollow eyes toward Rebecca. She squeaked and the thing moved through the flames like a ghost and descended upon her. They were eye-to-eye, the creature examining her carefully.

"Rebecca," I whispered, "don't move. Brett, give me your lighter."

From behind me: "Why?"

"Just. Do. It."

I reached inside my coat pocket hoping I might find something flammable.

A crumpled grocery receipt grazed my fingertips. Yes.

I extended my other hand behind me, palm up, expecting Brett's lighter.

From Rebecca's throat I could hear tiny whimpers and squeaks, and I could see sweat breaking out on her forehead. Her eyes were closed. The thing was inches from her face, moving like silk in the wind. It drew its face down the length of her body and stopped at her belly. And my God was it *smelling--?*

Smooth, cool plastic hit my palm. Slowly, I withdrew the grocery receipt.

"Hey," I said, and with a flick of the flint wheel, summoned a tiny flame. I touched that tiny flame to the receipt. The paper suddenly grew an orange crown.

It wasn't the quick attention grabber I'd hoped it would be.

The creature continued to examine Rebecca's abdomen with an animal-like curiosity. Its spindly, wispy fingers began whirling into thin vortexes, like four little tornadoes. They were shaping into talons. It opened its mouth (*there it is,* The Scream), and dozens of smoky fangs dropped from above and thrust from below like instantly forming stalactites and stalagmites. The curiosity left its face, replaced by satisfaction. Its spinning fingers were tapering off and solidifying into horrific weapons, claws sharp and strong enough to shred through cowhide, through human flesh. Ridiculously, *"when Skynet goes live"* popped into my head and I couldn't help but think of the T-1000 shape-shifting his limbs into deadly tools of murder.

It was time to be more assertive.

"Hey!" Louder this time.

Slowly, and seemingly against its own will, the thing drew its haunted gaze upwards at my flaming receipt. With grace, it lifted into the air, resembling both a giant black raven and a thundercloud, and came to rest in front of me. Unintentionally it grazed one of its sharp tornado fingers across Rebecca's face and left behind a red slash. She cried out but still did not move.

It made no eye contact with me. It was fully engaged,

bewitched, hypnotized by the flame, which was quickly burning down the receipt and closer to my fingers. Something would have to happen soon but all I could think was *I should have made more purchases!*

The next string of events happened so quickly I barely had time to process it all until I was running home.

The firelight glinted off the head of the axe as it came down. Only it wasn't an axe, it was a snow shovel. Brett swung it as if he were chopping wood. The blade of the shovel sliced perfectly through the smoky black body of the thing and then stopped abruptly midway through. Its body seemed to *grab* it, the shovel lodged in what served as the creature's abdomen. A sound like something out of a monster movie came from its gaping mouth. I'd heard a mountain lion screaming in the night once, and that is the closest comparison; like a woman-beast shrieking in pain, or pleasure. The particles of its body froze around the shovel blade and Brett immediately let go of the handle in amazement.

The fire finally ran out of receipt paper and singed my fingers. I hissed through clenched teeth and dropped the receipt as the creature quickly separated in two, like a dividing cell. The spell broke and the girls started screaming. The half of the creature's body containing the shovel fell to the earth with a wet thud and a metallic clang while the other half, the *still-alive* half, took to the sky with a banshee-wail that chilled me to my core. It flew to the far side of the yard, touched down in the snow for an instant, recovered, and crawled back over the fence. It continued howling as it retreated into the dark of the winter night and was joined by dozens of neighborhood dogs. Porch and patio lights turned on as concerned neighbors stepped outside to see what was making the awful sound.

I looked down at the discarded half. It was already a wet black ooze, like fresh tar.

"What the *crap* was that?" screamed Truffles, his voice cracking like a pubescent boy's.

Rebecca crumbled and Brett quickly reached out to catch her.

It knew.

It could smell *it somehow.*

It knew Rebecca was pregnant.

And it wanted what was inside.

Like a million sirens in my head, I was suddenly shocked by one singular thought:

Mom.

"I gotta go," I said in a daze and turned to go inside.

"Wait! What is happening?" called Truffles after me but the sirens muffled his words.

I blasted through Rebecca's house and flew out the front door, slipping on ice and completely forgetting about my own shovel. I ran as fast as I could down the middle of the street, fleeing the Raddock Addition like it was a house on fire (only, that expression wouldn't really apply to me). I ate shit once, completely losing my footing on a particularly thick and snow-shrouded patch of ice, and landed face-first in the street. I picked myself up and kept going, never mind my scraped-up palms and the gash on my chin now oozing blood down my neck. The frigid air bit my lungs with every gasp. And then there it was, our house you could see from Mars. I rounded the corner and turned on an extra bit of speed running up the last sixty feet or so of street.

I cut through our front yard, tromping through deep snow, then stopped cold.

A part of me knew it would be here.

Waiting.

Smaller now after discarding half its body, the black mass of it was huddled in the shadowy corner of the front porch. It was trembling.

It knows where I live. The recognition in its face hadn't just been my imagination.

It issued a series of high-pitched whines as if it were begging to be let inside.

I exhaled a stale breath and it lingered in the air, white and heavy.

The black mass turned to look at me.

I took a full two seconds to register that it wasn't the thing at all as it came bounding eagerly toward me. During those two seconds, it occurred to me that I should run but I knew it would only chase me, and the likelihood that I would outrun it was slim to none. So that was that. Final confrontation. One of us wouldn't be making it out alive.

Bright eyes. Lolling tongue. Big smile.

Equal parts shock and relief washed over me like an ocean wave refreshing the shoreline. Chloe had come home.

CHAPTER SIX

Where Chloe had been for the past four days we never learned. From her appearance, she'd not found an alternative home; she looked thinner, and her fur was dirty and matted with small snowballs that clung to her belly and haunches like white berries. Mom stopped in the middle of making dinner and immediately drew a bath. Lilly, tears of joy coursing down her cheeks, had her arms wrapped around Chloe's neck in a death lock. It was all Mom could do to tear her away so she could get Chloe into the tub. And normally, our shepherd hated baths, but as I watched her sitting obediently in the water with Mom and Lilly gently massaging shampoo into her fur, it looked as though Chloe could not care less. She seemed grateful to be back, surrounded by her family who loved her.

Chloe's homecoming momentarily shadowed the night's other events, and for that, I was grateful. It wasn't until Dad came home from work that I gave attention to the horrors from the evening at Rebecca's. The moment they struck me, Mom was toweling off Chloe, who spotted Dad as he came around the corner and bolted out of Mom's grip and ran to him. Dad, taken off guard, was at once confused but quickly fell back into the familiar doggie embrace of paws on chest and tongue kisses.

"She was waiting at the front door," I said. "Found her way home."

Dad registered my wan smile and held his eyes on me for a few seconds longer.

He knew right away there was more to this evening than Chloe's return.

"I should get back to dinner," Mom announced cheerily, clapping her hands together. "Lilly, will you please feed Chloe? And pour a can of gravy over her kibble, we need to fatten her up."

"Come on, girl," said Lilly, with so much excitement you'd think Christmas had come a week early. She and Chloe scampered off to the garage.

"Dan," said Dad. "Help me bring in some firewood, will ya?" He flashed me a knowing look. As Mom went to the kitchen, she gave Dad a smooch on the cheek.

"Dinner will be ready in forty-five," she said.

"Okay, love."

"I'm putting on some Christmas music, it feels like we should celebrate."

"Where's Soren?"

"Pizza with friends."

"Curfew?"

"I told him be home by nine."

Dad nodded, satisfied with her answer despite the tension still present on his face.

"And, boys," started Mom in a quieter voice, "let's keep the Oopsie under wraps for a few more days, okay?" She looked

Dad in the eye. "And please have a conversation with your son about respecting his mother." She looked at me and smiled. As she entered the kitchen, she hummed the tune to "Sleigh Ride." Dad gave me a hard sideways stare and sighed. For a second I thought he was going to tear into me, but instead his eyes turned toward the window to look upon the wintery night. Beautiful patterns of frost were forming at the edges of the glass. The light from our million-watt Christmas house illuminated the gentle snowfall. Somewhere out in the darker reaches of the night, shadows moved and glided past houses and fences.

"Come on," said Dad.

I told him everything from start to finish (minus the part where I drank a beer) and he listened intently to every detail without a show of emotion. Dad was always good at hiding his stronger feelings like fear and sadness, but his stoicism was a telltale sign that my story scared him. He chewed on the inside of his lip as his gloved hands stacked another log in my arms.

"It's like," I continued, "like...wherever it came from has different physical laws than our world's laws. It can't remain a solid—*thing*—without coming in constant contact with other solid things. The shovel almost sliced right through it until... its body *grabbed* it, like it took a second for its particles or whatever to vibrate faster and harden."

Dad grinned. "You sound smarter than you look."

"I get it from Mom's side."

"Smartass."

"Our world doesn't support its existence, Dad, it's not supposed to be here."

"Obviously."

"And it eats—" I struggled to complete the sentence even though I knew what to say.

"I know."

"We're telling Mom."

"Daniel—"

"Dad, I saw it—*up close*. I saw what it wanted."

"Just slow down for a second, Dan, okay? I'd rather talk about getting rid of it. Killing it."

An unexpected pang of disapproval at Dad's words struck me and took me completely off guard to the point that I missed the next thing he said.

"Right, Dan?"

"What?"

"Let's take care of the problem before it becomes a problem."

I shook the odd feeling away and refocused. "Yeah. But Mom needs to be warned, she's pregnant."

"A fact I thought I told you to keep between you and me."

"Well, she pissed me off."

"And now we're both in trouble. Happy?"

"Dad, if she knew *why* you told me, it wouldn't be a big deal! We'd be protecting her!"

He stacked another log in my arms.

"Okay, that's all I can handle, my muscles are gonna pop."

Dad palmed two wood blocks and gave a nod for me to go inside.

"All right," he said with a weary sigh, "we'll tell her. Tonight, after Soren and Lilly are in bed. But I want to focus on finding it and catching it as soon as possible. I want it gone. I'll get Henry to help us."

We started toward the house. "It's not an animal, Dad, we don't need a dog catcher, we need the Ghostbusters or something."

"We just need to lure it in," said Dad. "Just like trapping any animal."

I had to grin. Oh, the irony. "That I think I can help with."

"Fire."

Mom, Dad and I sat in the den in front of a low burning, popping fire in the fireplace. The wrinkle between Mom's eyebrows had not smoothed out since Dad and I launched into our respective stories involving the thing, and she'd begun to nervously chew on the inside of her cheek. She remained quiet throughout and I couldn't tell if she was processing the quite literally *unbelievable* information we were delivering or if she was waiting for the punch line to an unfunny joke. It seemed the latter was more the case. Everything we were saying sounded like a work of fiction ripped from the Stephen King library. The only thing keeping her from calling our bluff was the known fact that neither Dad nor I were pranksters. We were not a family of practical jokers. The only pranks ever played were usually between Soren and I, and rarely did Mom ever find out about those. She took a sip of water (wishing, I'm sure, that it was a drink much stronger) and asked how on earth we mere mortals planned on finding, capturing, and destroying a supernatural entity. And I'd not missed a beat in my response.

Mom laughed. "Okay, now I know you're joking, and I have to tell you both something: it's not funny."

"Mom, I know it sounds crazy, I know it does, but—"

"Which part? The part about an otherworldly ghost monster that eats babies, or the part where fire—*fire*—is your one solution to finding it, Daniel, because I'd like to be clear on what part you think sounds crazy."

Dad leaned forward and laid a hand on Mom's knee. "Sweetheart, listen to me. I've seen what this thing can do and it is not a joke. My God, I wish it were. It's the reason Chloe ran away, it's what ripped Bert Wickstrom's springers open—"

"And attacked the Tomlinsons," I added.

"I thought you said that was a coyote."

"Mom, think about it: would a coyote jump through a window and attack two elderly people for no apparent reason? Does that sound like coyote behavior to you?"

"So why did your...*thing* do it, huh?"

I'd thought about this and come to only one conclusion that made any kind of sense. "The Tomlinsons' Christmas tree was all red lights. Red: like fire. Maybe it was curious enough to break through the window."

Mom took a breath like she was about to say something, but it came out as a short laugh, and she shook her head.

"You understand why I'm having trouble with this, right? It's like asking me to believe in Santa Claus."

"Actually, the devil is more appropriate," I said.

"Whatever. You both sound nuts. I'm not sure I believe you, but I believe that *you* believe there is something out there." She paused, looked us both square in the eye. "So. What's your plan?"

I looked at Dad as if he already had the answer, as if he'd

been given enough time to already formulate a plan. As it happened, he had.

"I have an idea," he said.

The following afternoon found Dad, Animal Control Henry, and I out at Bert Wickstrom's ranch. I feared I'd see remnants of dead springer carnage in the field, but of course the cow corpses had been hauled away and the red snow had been buried beneath a fresh layer. Bert wore the remnants on his face, however: dark bags nearly swallowing his beady ash-colored eyes, pale complexion causing the liver spots to pop, and a wrinkly frown that made me wonder if I'd ever see old Bert walk through the door to our AA meeting and smile again. No doubt he'd lost sleep over this. Plus, the undertaking of disposing the dead springers had to have aged his already aged body by a few precious years. At first, I thought Dad's plan was the last thing Bert would want to participate in, but once Dad explained to him his idea, he was unquestioningly on board. It didn't seem to matter that the subject of our imprisonment plot was a sci-fi/horror-fantasy creature from God-Knows-Where. Bert was salivating for revenge.

He and my father were smoothing out an area map of Ferdinand on Bert's giant dining room table when I felt a tap on my shoulder.

"So, Danny," said Henry, with a wrinkled brow and a hand on his hip, elbow cocked. "How is it that *fire* is gonna lure this —*thing*—into Bert's horse trailer? I'd think proper bait, like what it eats, would be better." He looked genuinely confused as if I'd explained it in a foreign language.

"We are not using my wife as bait, Henry," said Dad. "And by the way, don't let on that you know, she'll kill me."

"I don't think my friend Rebecca would be too eager either," I said. "Besides, we don't need them for bait. This thing...with fire, it's like a bug to a light. It's attracted to it. I've seen it. For whatever reason, it finds fire fascinating."

Henry grinned maliciously. "Like a bug-zapper."

"Yeah, I guess," I said.

"But why? Why fire?"

I searched Henry's expression for any trace of suspicion. If I were him, I'd be seriously questioning this whole cocka-mamie plan and the odd connection it had to a known pyro too. But as it was, perhaps Henry had no memory or knowl-edge of my blazing reputation and was simply asking a perfectly reasonable question of the boy who seemed to have the most information.

"I don't know why," I said. "Maybe, wherever it comes from, there is no fire. It's never seen fire before. And so it finds it new and strange and pretty and...irresistible. Or maybe fire is the one familiar thing it has in our world, and seeing it reminds it of home."

Henry regarded me as if I'd just confessed that I some-times wear women's clothes and go by the name Danielle: disapproving but wanting to remain PC about it.

"Yep, well, ah-yep, that's..." he trailed off.

And right then, I realized that I sympathized with this sci-fi/horror-fantasy creature from God-Knows-Where. It was why I felt a strange aversion to the idea of killing it.

This newly fathomed revelation could pose a serious problem.

"Hey Dan," said Dad, nodding me over, "come here."

I left Henry with a contemplative look on his face and huddled with Dad and Bert over the area map. Bert's aftershave tickled my nose.

"Rebecca's house is whereabouts?" asked Dad, a black Sharpie in his hand, poised over the map. There were already four Xs marked on various locations; locations, I noted, that were alarmingly close to our house. I pointed to a spot in the Raddock Addition. Dad made a fifth X. He and Bert leaned slightly out to get a better perspective. Henry leaned in.

"Okay," started Dad. He made a big black circle that ran through the five X's. "Bert, it looks like your ranch was an anomaly. It's pretty far from where this thing seems to have made its territory. If we were to triangulate where to set our trap, it's gonna be in here." He made a smaller circle within the bigger one.

"Yup," said Bert.

"Looks like a central location is here," said Henry, placing his finger in the middle of the smaller circle. "Who lives here?"

Bert shook his head. "Nah. That's ol' Juniper's field. He's got horses. An' he's an asshole."

"Bert's right. June wouldn't go for it," Dad agreed.

"Could he be persuaded?"

Dad pressed his lips together and capped the Sharpie. "The fewer people involved, the better."

"In that case…" said Bert, thrusting three callused fingers down on the map in lieu of a forefinger, which was no more than a nub. Every time I saw that missing finger, I couldn't help but imagine what a grizzly end it came to, victim to a combine. The tip of his middle fingernail was covering where our house would be. Dad's eyes shifted gravely to Bert's withered face.

"No, Bert, I don't want that thing around my house."

"It already is!" said Bert, his dusty voice cracking. With his finger he traced the black circle Dad had made. "If we're talkin' territory, your house looks like Ground Zero to me."

"Ben, doesn't your backyard fence have a swinging gate?" said Henry. "We could pull the horse trailer right through there."

"It's not wide enough for a trailer," said Dad.

"You back your pickup through there every fall so's you can unload yer firewood, right? That trailer ain't wider than the bed of your pickup. It's a single-horse Kingston, would slip through your gate no problem."

"It puts my family at risk."

"Ain't they already at risk?"

"And my neighbors? You don't think they won't be asking why we've got a barbecue grill on fire and a horse trailer in my backyard?"

"Dad, most of our neighbors are out of town for Christmas. I know. I shovel their stupid driveways," I said.

"Starting a fire like that in a residential area is going to attract attention. Might even be dangerous."

"You got Juniper's field right behind you, ain't nothin' but snow and a couple apple trees. Houses to left and right, but Benny, we can manage a little fire."

"And when the cops come?"

"I'll handle them," said Henry. "Dean and Arnie are good buddies of mine."

Bert fixed my dad with a stern eye. "Seems yer runnin' outta excuses, Benjamin."

Dad shook his head, his expression resolute: *It's not going to happen, gentlemen.* But then he looked up from the area map and right into my eyes. His face softened (and maybe I was the only one who saw it), and his steely blue eyes searched mine. He was looking for my approval. My vote.

There were maybe two or three other moments in my life before and after this one that felt like an ushering into adulthood, when the child has finally earned his space among respected elders and is seen as an equal man. When our parents are no longer flawless caregivers and teachers and disciplinarians and safety nets but people, lost and searching for the right answer like the rest of us.

I gave him a nod.

Dad looked at the other two men. "Okay. My house."

"Everything will be fine, Benny, you'll see," said Henry.

"Okay, second order of business," Dad continued. "We need to secure the trailer. Board up the windows and any open slats, except for the one above the hitch, of course, those bullet-holes, Bert, what the hell were you using it for, target practice? We save that last window till last minute. But any other holes gotta be covered, no matter how small. The way I understand it, this thing could squeeze its way through a keyhole if it wanted to."

"I got a pile of two-by-fours sittin' out back we can screw right over the winda's," offered Bert. "That gonna do it?"

The men looked at Dad. Dad looked at me.

On the spot, all I could do was shrug. "I hope," I squeaked with a little more panic in my voice than I'd wanted to project. "I mean, it has claws but I don't think it's strong enough to bust through a two-by-four. I think it's hurt pretty bad right now. But honestly, I only know a little more about this thing than you guys do."

Dad took a deep breath. "He's right. We don't know what this thing is capable of and there are a hundred different things that could go wrong. We just have to be as prepared as we can be. Bert, how long you suppose it'll take to secure the trailer?"

"All of us screwing in boards and caulking up holes and such, prolly no more'n a couple hours."

Dad folded up the map. "You got a piece of scratch paper, Bert? I wanna draw this out."

Bert disappeared into the living room momentarily. Out the window was a crisp winter day, the sky the purest, sharpest blue that only winter skies can produce. The fresh powder sparkled too brightly and left a green ghost behind my eyelids. Luckily, there was no snow in the forecast, which was fortunate for our operation. Having complete visibility would be important. We were pitting ourselves against a force none of us understood and any help from Mother Nature was most welcomed.

Bert returned with a sheet of 8x11 printer paper and a sharpened No. 2 pencil. Dad took the pencil between forefinger and thumb and slapped the paper down on the dining table.

"Okay, I'm no artist but this'll help…" He drew a box with soft corners. At one end, on either side of the box, he drew two smaller, upward-slanting boxes. "Okay. The trailer has two doors that swing outward. That's these." He tapped the pencil point against the two upward-slanting boxes. "We'll put a guy behind each door." Dad drew two little stick figures positioned behind the swinging trailer doors. "One guy will be in charge of feeding the fire." In front of the trailer he drew a circle with a horizontal line through the middle and three legs coming down in tripod formation. On the bottom of the legs, he drew three little circles. Next to the "barbecue grill" he drew another stick figure. His last touch was a jagged series of triangles coming out of the circle like a child would draw a mountain range. "That's the fire. Obviously, the lid won't be on but...whatever." He cleared his throat. "There's a ramp—" In three swift flourishes Dad drew a right-angled triangle at the base of the trailer— "upon which one of us will be pulling the grill into the trailer, by a rope, which we'll feed through that back window above the hitch." He drew a line extending from the grill through the trailer and out the other end. "Once the thing sees the fire and takes the bait, the guy by the hitch will pull on the rope and wheel the grill up the ramp and into the trailer." He connected the line from the grill to the hands of a crouched stick figure behind the hitch. "Once inside, the door guys will yank away the ramp and slam the doors shut. Then rope guy will cut the rope or throw the slack inside and quickly board up the rear window."

Bert and Henry stared at the drawing and nodded their heads as they digested the plan.

"Then what?" I asked. "We have it trapped. Then what?"

"The way I see it," started Dad, "it's just like any animal. We know it eats, right? We know it's had to eat to survive here. Once it's trapped inside the trailer, we just wait. We starve it out. We starve it until it dies or disintegrates or whatever the hell it does. No one tries to kill it, no one even has to go *near* it. It starves, it dies, the end."

That pang of empathy needled my chest again and I looked

away so Dad couldn't see. I pretended to look back at the drawing.

"Seems like a lot for one man," said Bert, pointing to the stick figure pulling on the rope. "Seconds count. Be better to have another man with a board and drill at the ready, dontcha think?"

"We won't have another man, Bert. The fewer the better, remember?"

"Bert is right, Benny," Henry chimed in. "I think having a fifth man there is a good idea. Like you said, a hundred different things could go wrong. Wouldn't it be nice to have another set of hands in case something did?"

Dad set the pencil down. It rolled a few inches across the page. "Getting someone else involved who hasn't seen what this thing can do, who might look at us and think we're a bunch of wack-a-doos is...precarious. Who's gonna believe us? Moreover, who can we *trust* who's gonna believe us? I know this feels like a slapdash operation but I'm not treating it like one."

"Then let's get one more guy, Ben," said Henry. "Someone we do trust. Someone who does know what this thing can do."

"Who's that, Henry? Far as I know, all the people aware of what we're dealing with—a goddamn supernatural being—are in this room."

"That's not true," I said.

"Daniel, we are not under any circumstances involving your mother—"

"Not Mom. Someone else. Someone I trust. Someone who has seen what this thing can do."

. . .

While Dad and the others prepared the horse trailer, I got permission to drive Dad's truck for my recruitment mission. It hadn't been that long since my driving privileges were revoked, but those twenty minutes driving back to town felt fresh and revitalizing, like being behind the wheel was an old friend and we'd just been gleefully reunited. Despite the wintry cold, I drove with the window down but the heat cranked to max and reveled in the wind on my skin and in my hair.

With the bluest blue sky above me, the clean fresh powder blanketing the fields around me, the brisk blast of air filling my lungs and ruffling my jacket collar, and the feel of a V-6 engine at my command, life felt awfully close to normal again. It wouldn't occur to me until much later, but in that moment, I didn't even crave a drink; not a beer, not a whiskey ginger, nothing. I was okay. And it wouldn't occur to me until much, much later how important that was.

I pulled Dad's truck alongside the curb outside of Truffles' house. There were cars in the driveway, so I assumed he was home. I suppose I could have just called him, but a face-to-face conversation is what this situation warranted. Plus, with Truffles, you sort of had to ambush him with a plan. Otherwise, nine times out of ten, he would say no, and with this particular operation, no was not an option.

I gave three sturdy knocks on the door. Small dogs within lit up with the kind of yapping that made you want to show them the steel toe of your boot. Seconds later the door flew open and, lo and behold, behind it was the very man I came to see. He was too worried about keeping the tiny yipping creatures away from the crack in the door to notice who'd even knocked. When he finally kicked them sufficiently away and looked up, his face registered a close encounter with the Wolfman instead of a longtime friend.

"Danny," he said, nearly breathless. The dogs continued to yatter behind him.

"Hey, Truff."

"Dude, what the crap?!"

"I know, I know—"

"That *thing*—and then—holy shit—but then you ran off and—I haven't slept 'cause I can't get it out of my head and—Jesus H, and Rebecca freaked out—SHUT UP, BROWNIE!—and then that blob—what the shit??—what's going on, man?"

"Truffles, calm down, okay?"

He squeezed his bulk through the crack in the door and joined me on the porch step, leaving the maddening terriers to bark themselves to death.

"Calm down? Are you serious?"

"Before you ask questions I don't have answers to, just listen for a minute, okay? Will you just listen to me?"

Truffles' slack jaw stayed slack, but he took a breath and leaned back on his heels, acquiescing.

"I don't know what it is, I don't know where it came from. I know that it eats babies, the younger the better. Species doesn't seem to matter. And it—" I paused, thinking of a different way to word this but came up empty—"is drawn to fire."

I was expecting a guffaw, maybe a groan or an eye roll at the least. Where Henry might not have known my history, Truffles certainly did. He was a part of it.

"Yeah, and...?" responded Truffles with not a trace of sarcasm, suspicion, or belittlement. His fretful eyes searched me for conclusion.

"And…we're gonna use that to trap it."

"Okay, great! Crazy, but great!"

"And we need your help."

Truffles' raised shoulders and eyebrows both dropped like a puppet's. His tone followed suit. "What?"

"We have a plan—well, my dad has a plan actually, and I think it's pretty good, but we're a man short and since you've seen this *thing* and kinda know—"

"Dan—"

"I know it's crazy, I know it *sounds* crazy but Truffles, you gotta trust me—"

"I don't wanna get anywhere *near* that thing—"

"Didn't you see it with Rebecca? It wanted to cut her open—"

"Which is why I don't want to go near it!"

"That doesn't matter! It's out there, in your town—in *our* town—and—"

"I feel like I'm going crazy here, like I'm dreaming or something—"

"And someone is gonna get hurt, seriously hurt, maybe *dead* if we don't do something…"

"Dan, I have to go." Truffles reached behind himself for the doorknob.

"Truffles, please, wait—"

"I'm not the guy for the job, you know that, you know how I am—"

"Stop, please—"

"Tomorrow is Christmas Eve, Dan, and I'd like to be alive for it." Truffles turned the knob. Just the clicking sound was enough to set the terriers off again. "SHUT UP, BROWNIE! You should find someone else."

"I don't have anyone else," I said. It came out so quickly, so truthfully that I was taken off guard by my own admittance. I felt my face flush.

Truffles' hand dropped from the doorknob.

Is that true? Has my friend list been reduced to one? I honestly hadn't given it much thought since this whole thing started and now, in this oddly desperate moment, it hit me like when you miss a step down and your stomach drops for an instant and you look around to see if anyone saw you stumble like an idiot. I could think of a few friends I'd had to leave behind at the university, but according to my AA counselor, people who were exclusively drinking buddies were not real friends.

The look on Truffles' face made me harden. I didn't need his pity. But I suddenly had a foot in the door, so I went with it.

"You're the best friend I got, Truffles, you're the *only* friend. I know I've dragged you into some shit before...but this isn't like those times. This isn't about me making trouble or trying to have fun at someone else's expense. This is about stopping something before anyone else gets hurt. This is about making a difference and putting other people before ourselves. Yes, it's gonna be dangerous. And no, I have no clue what's gonna happen. And no, I can't guarantee your safety. But no one is gonna stop this thing unless we do it. You're the only person I can trust here, Truffles. After all we've been through, I hope you can still trust me. Please. I need you."

Truffles stared at me with sympathy and incredulity in equal parts but mostly he looked like I'd just fed him a bunch of bullshit and he was waiting to call me on it.

"Nice speech," he said.

"Thanks. I was thinking of ending it with 'Today...we celebrate…our Independence Day' but thought that might be overdoing it."

Truffles' skepticism cracked into a smile. I smiled back.

"Please, Truffles," I said earnestly. "This won't work without you."

Truffles' eyes slowly narrowed. He let out an unnecessarily long sigh.

"You're a pain in the ass, you know that, Daniel?" he said.

"I know. I'm sorry."

"How in the hell did you get wrapped up in this?"

"It's a long story. I'll tell you the whole thing start to finish if you help us."

Another unnecessarily long sigh. *Jesus, Truff, I get it already.*

"If I have to run, I'm fucked. You know I'm slow and have asthma."

"If everything goes according to plan—"

"Which it never does—"

"If everything goes according to plan, you shouldn't have to run." I paused for a second. "Besides…I think it's as afraid of us as we are of it. Or at least it should be."

While he internally deliberated, Truffles' focus went down to the snowy front lawn, then shifted to some faraway street sign, and lastly, angled up toward the heavens. He shook his head as if this were the part in a movie where some guardian angel or dead relative that'd been saying, "You can do this, just believe in yourself," was finally given validation with a, "You were right you ol' rascal, I should have listened to you before 'cause you're dead (or an angel), ergo, you know what's best for me."

"This is nuts," he started, his eyes widening and his

expression taking on the look of a parent who is reprimanding a petulant child, "but okay. Tell me this plan of yours."

By 5:20 p.m. on December 23rd the trap was set. It'd been a tiny struggle to get the trailer through the fence after all, but with deft maneuvering behind the wheel, courtesy of my pa Benjamin, it squeaked through with little to no damage. I think I heard the phrase, "Put 'er in four-wheel drive," followed by, "Jesus Christ, it is!" about eighteen times before Dad's pickup made it into the backyard, delivered the payload, and then, tires spinning on slick snow-packed tracks, finally made it back to the paved street.

The horse trailer, with its recently added security measures, looked like something built in preparation for the zombie apocalypse or to transport a velociraptor. The slats through which a horse would normally receive light and a nice breeze were boarded up with sturdy two-by-fours, fastened into the metal with thick screws. All other holes (screw holes, rust-eaten holes, bullet-holes, etc.) were either welded and/or boarded, except of course for the back window through which Dad would be pulling the rope attached to the grill. I stared at the trailer sitting in our backyard with its opened double doors and couldn't help but imagine several walking dead being herded inside. Or breaking out.

Dad laid a large sheet of plywood in front of the ramp leading up to the mouth of the trailer. I thought it would be a good idea to have the fire as visible as possible from all sides and every angle, and so, to have it set away from the trailer as far as we could manage. With the rope tied to two of the grill legs, Dad practiced pulling it across the plywood, up the ramp, and into the trailer. During the third dry run, the grill got stuck on the lip between the plywood and the ramp and nearly tipped over.

"Gentle, Dad, gentle," I coaxed.

"I hear ya. I know," he said calmly, but I could plainly hear frustration in his voice.

I watched as the grill, looking like a black Death Star on three legs or one of the alien tripods from "War of the Worlds," teetered on the lip of the ramp. After a light but consistent pull on the rope, the wheels finally climbed up onto the ramp, and Dad and I breathed a collective sigh of relief.

"Dad?"

He set the rope down and came out from behind the trailer. "Yes, son?"

"What if it doesn't work?"

Dad looked out into Juniper's field. The daylight was fading fast, the remnants of it painting the world an icy cavern blue. Snow-covered trees took on a blueberry hue while the moonlit ground sparkled like sapphires. The very air itself seemed colored to match the coldest shades of the ocean.

Dad raised his eyebrows. "All things are possible."

Unsatisfied with his dismissive, Taoist rhetoric, I said, "No, like, what if it doesn't come? I think we might have hurt it pretty bad before with the shovel. What if it now associates fire with...pain? What if it recognizes fire as something bad now? What if it recognizes...me?"

Dad took a deep breath and released it in a thick cloud. He cupped my shoulder and pulled me warmly into a side hug. "Then we'll just think of something else."

Most of me was taken aback by the sudden affection but the small rest of me welcomed it.

"Daniel, I..." he started.

I gave him my attention. It sounded like he was about to open up about something.

"—think we should get inside."

He gave my shoulder a pat and released me.

"Yeah," I said, covering the fact that I was expecting something else and followed him into the house.

Before dinner, I overheard a conversation between Mom and Dad. I was coming out of my bedroom and noticed their door slightly ajar, low voices speaking privately behind it. It sounded like it was mostly Dad who didn't want to make this conversation a family affair so, naturally, I eavesdropped.

Dad's voice came first. "After you drop off Lilly and Soren you're going to Erica's, and I don't want to hear another word about it."

Mom: "I am not leaving, Ben, and quick reminder: Erica and I haven't spoken in over a year."

"Well, you're not staying here. It's too dangerous."

"Why do men assume they're the only heroes in stories, huh? What if you need me to come to *your* rescue?"

"I *do* need you. You are the most important thing in my life, I am not losing you again, which is why you can't be here."

"I love you Benjamin, but you're crazy if you think I'm leaving—"

"Christ, Renee, we know two things about this thing: it's attracted to fire and it eats unborn babies. It will *kill* you both if it smells you."

"So we won't let it *smell* me! Whatever this *thing* is, I am not leaving my husband and son to fight it alone. Soren and

Lilly will be safe. But I'm staying. I'm sorry if you disagree, but I've made up my mind and you're going to have to call Officer Tackett to drag my body kicking and screaming from this house if you want me gone."

I heard the stubble-scratch of Dad running his hands down the front of his face in frustration. "Jesus, I married a brick wall."

"I'll keep inside," Mom continued, "I'll just keep watch."

"Stay away from the doors and windows. Keep lights off. Silence, Renee. Don't make a sound."

"It won't even know I'm here. Plus, I'll have Chloe to protect me."

"She ran away from it, remember?"

"Then she'll have me to protect her."

Dad sighed, long and heavy. Then, "You're a fucking nightmare, you know that?"

"One from which you're never gonna wake." I could hear the smile in Mom's voice.

Dad kissed her. "And I never want to."

Bert and Henry had both gone home after situating the trailer, wanting to rest up in case there was a long night ahead, but returned around 7:30. Bert wore a thick wool-lined coat and a pair of Wranglers that made the poor man's legs look skinny as uncooked spaghetti noodles, and a Stetson cowboy hat. Henry donned a black and gray fleece jacket and a knitted cap that looked handmade (probably by his wife Betsy, an avid and fiercely competitive member of the local ladies' Crochet Club).

Mom handed both Bert and Henry steaming mugs of strong black coffee.

"Thanks, Renee," they said in unison.

"How are things, Bert?" she asked, lifting her own mug to her lips.

"Nothing to grumble at," he replied, which couldn't seem less of an understatement given the odd bounce in his usually stoic step. He wasn't cheerful per se, but definitely *lifted*, as if he were about to cunningly hunt down a long-time nemesis, some chicken-killing raccoon or a bothersome fox that deserved his sweet and chilling vengeance. He sipped his coffee and regarded the rest of us like he was attending a Christmas party, coffee spiked with Bailey's and a night of carefree holiday frivolity ahead of him. Henry couldn't have been more opposite: no smile, no contribution to the conversation, just taking constant tiny slurps of his coffee to avoid engaging his mouth and voice. Once or twice his lips jerked into a grin, but it seemed obligatory. He was scared, I could tell.

Because so was I.

I'd noticed it when he first walked in, but Chloe was the one who drew attention to the double-action revolver holstered at Bert's waist. Curious about all the visitors, she'd gone around sniffing shoes and fingertips and crotches, as dogs are inclined to do, and stopped at a particularly different smell when she'd reached Bert's gun.

"What's that for?" I asked.

Bert followed my eyes and gave both the gun and Chloe a friendly pat. "Just precaution."

"No disrespect, Mr. Wickstrom, but I don't think a gun

will help," I said genuinely. "A bullet is too fast, it'll go right through it and not do a thing."

"I carry this everywhere, son. Might not do us good tonight, but if it does, you'll be glad I have it," said Bert, spoken like the true conservative card-carrying member of the NRA that he was.

The conversation might have continued if the doorbell hadn't rung. As I went to welcome Truffles, Bert asked, "So where are your youngest?"

Mom said, "Away. Spending the night with friends."

"Pro'lly a good idea."

"No doubt." I could hear the distaste in her tone. She didn't like guns either.

Truffles' uneasy smile and nervous eyes were almost comical as the first thing to greet me behind the front door.

"Hey," he said, "I'm here."

I grinned. "Yes, you are."

"Am I late?"

"Actually, you're right on time. Come on in."

Truffles entered at the same time Dad came down the hallway from the bedroom. He was guarded against the winter night by a downy North Face jacket and navy-blue cotton scarf. A sturdy thick pair of cowhide gloves, the ones he wore when chopping and stacking wood in the fall, protected his hands. He gave Truffles a nod.

"Hello there, Desmond," he said, using Truffles' real name, a name I hadn't heard anyone call him, well, ever. Not even teachers called him Desmond.

"Hello, sir." Ever the respectful young man.

Dad regarded the room.

"Well fellas, should we get on with it?"

Bert and Henry set their mugs down and pulled on their gloves. I retrieved my own North Face jacket and wool cap.

Here we go.

Despite the moon glow, our backyard was darker than a usual night in December. We'd opted to keep the outdoor Christmas lights off in case they would pollute the darkness and hinder the effectiveness of attracting the *thing* to our fire. The night sky was clear and black, the billion radiant stars sharp enough to slice open the atmosphere were they to fall. The cold burned in our lungs and froze our nose hairs. I was sure if I didn't continuously blink, a skim of ice would form over my eyeballs and I'd see the world through opaque lenses.

"Well, we've got ourselves one helluva mousetrap, eh gents?" said Bert as we crunched our way toward the trailer.

A pile of kindling lay beside the sheet of plywood with a hearty stack already within the grill. Dad had placed a can of lighter fluid next to it. When we reached the trailer, Dad withdrew a pack of matches from his pocket.

"You're in charge of the fire," he said to me, which at first I thought was a cruel joke but quickly realized he was being serious. He slapped the matchbook inside my palm. "I don't think there was ever a person more qualified to make sure this fire stays big and beautiful, for as long as it takes."

Before I could respond Dad turned away.

"Okay, fellas. Everyone listen up," he started. Truffles snapped to like a chatty soldier suddenly called to attention by his staff sergeant. "None of us really knows what we're in for tonight. I'm still trying to wrap my mind around it myself." He paused, took a heavy breath. There was just the tiniest bit of fear in his voice, barely perceptible, but it was there. Hearing it set loose a flurry of nerves deep in my belly. "Let me know if there are objections to my plan: Bert and I will be at the back window. I will be reeling in the grill and Bert will have the screw gun and two-by-four at the ready once the rope is cut. Henry, you and Desmond will be behind each door and latch them shut once the thing has cleared the threshold. One of you—Henry—will also need to flip up the ramp, but make sure the grill and the *thing* has cleared the space where the ramp falls, we don't want it getting in the way. If the ramp isn't secured in its proper position, the doors will not latch."

"Got it," said Henry.

"Daniel, you will be in charge of feeding the fire. If we need more kindling someone can volunteer to chop some more, I have plenty of firewood stacked up by the house. That fire must be kept as raging and as alive as we can keep it. Okay. Everyone know their stations?"

A collective "Yep" and "Mmhmm" issued from our odd little ragtag team.

"Okay then. Daniel."

Dad gave me a nod. I turned my gaze toward the wood-filled grill.

The grate upon which meats and vegetables would normally be grilled had been removed and the grill was now just a vessel for kindling. The lid had been stowed away in the garage; the Death Star bisected and stuffed with Douglas fir. I grabbed the can of lighter fluid and hosed down the kindling while Dad took Bert to the back of the trailer.

"Cut the rope with these," Dad said, picking up a pair of hedge trimmers. Bert nodded.

I tore a match out of the book and swiped it against the

strike strip. Bright orange flame burst from the match tip and flickered once or twice as it devoured the phosphorus, sulfur, and potassium chlorate. I caught Truffles eyeing me warily as I watched the tiny flame quiver and sway. And then, without further hesitation, I tossed it on the fluid-soaked kindling.

Whummp!

Like a bird unfolding its wings the fire came to life and reached for the stars. A spot of warmth melted the icy air, and instinctively we all took a step closer.

We had our bait. The trap was set. Now all we had to do was wait.

We executed a couple dry runs so Henry could practice flipping up and securing the ramp and both he and Truffles could close and bolt the doors. Both times, Truffles' sense of urgency was so on point he nearly took Henry's fingers off. Better to move hastily than not, I guessed. Milliseconds might count. From the wary look on his face, Henry might disagree.

And after that, we waited. Dad made idle conversation with Bert and Henry while I continued to feed our fire. It was a clean burn with very little smoke. The bright flames like liquid candy corn continued to lap at the frozen air, tasting the night.

"Have you talked to Nick lately?" asked Truffles out of the blue.

I looked up from the fire, scratched my head through my beanie. "No. Not since graduation."

"He's with his family in Arizona for Christmas. We text every so often," said Truffles with a touch of melancholy, as if "every so often" was a sad downgrade from the otherwise frequent communication they'd once shared. High school friends grow apart, that's just how it is, but Truffles was clearly having difficulty with this fact.

"We didn't talk much before graduation, actually," I said, suddenly feeling the same sadness. "He started going out with Kara our junior year and we…you know how it is…"

"Yeah. Bros-Before-Hoes didn't really apply to him, huh?"

I thought about the truth for a second. Considered not telling it. The truth stung and giving voice to it made it truer.

"Actually," I started, feeling that old regret pushing against my chest, "we didn't talk much after 'The House.' I think we just pretended everything was okay after that, but it wasn't."

With friends and family, after I'd razed the farmer's house to the ground, 'The House' became the name for the event, like '9/11' or 'Pearl Harbor' or 'Watergate.' Here are a few common sentences I heard in the aftermath of that event:

"Everything changed after 'The House.'"

"Bro, 'The House!' That was fuckin' EPIC!"

"Remember 'The House?' Remember being grounded afterward? I'll ground you twice *as long, young man!"*

Truffles nodded at the ground. "Yeah. I know. Nothing was the same after 'The House.' No offense."

I shifted my gaze back to the fire. "None taken," I said as I bent to grab another piece of wood. I laid it on the pyre.

Sometimes I truly missed Nick. He'd been my best friend. We always sort of looked out for one another.

But there was that day that our tight-knit friendship started to fray. Even before "The House." "The House" was the straw that broke the camel's back. But it was that day in late July that was the beginning of the end.

And in an instant, the disquieting memory of Nick, me, and the moth came surging back.

Nick's eyes.

It was Nick's eyes I remembered the most.

It had been another scorcher. Like fry-an-egg-on-the-sidewalk hot, like record temperatures hot. The whole state was praying for rain, but the inevitable fire season had already been set in motion; August was sure to be a smoky, hellish nightmare.

Mom and Dad hadn't separated yet, but they were on the brink. I think they got into more arguments that summer because of the heat. It made them all the more irritable.

I was still thirteen but weeks away from fourteen.

And my experimentation with fire was at an all-time high.

Nick was on his way over to my house. We were gonna beat the heat and spend the afternoon inside the cool, dark movie theater. J.J. Abrams' new flick *Super 8* had just come out and we were both dying to see it. At fourteen, Nick already considered himself a hardcore cinephile and said this movie was a throwback to the golden days of Spielberg and we had to see it in the theater or we'd regret it for the rest of our lives. But just the week before he'd said the same thing about *Pirates of the Caribbean: On Stranger Tides* and that movie sucked. Nevertheless, I trusted him, and was a fan of all the Abrams stuff he'd shown me, so *Super 8* was a big deal.

When he found me, I was in the backyard, shirtless and wearing board shorts, hunched over an opened matchbook with a magnifying glass in my hand. I was careful that the sweat dripping off my nose didn't soak the sulfur match tips.

Soren had recently gone through an odd but brief Sherlock Holmes phase where he wished to be exclusively referred to as

Soren Patrick: Kid Detective. Mom and Dad had supplied him with all the investigative accoutrements for his birthday and he'd obsessively searched for clues and drawn conclusions to imaginary cases for at least three-and-a-half months. But, as with all children, his imagination eventually ran dry of this particular game, and he sought out new scenarios to explore. I'd found the magnifying glass in his room one day, tossed aside and forgotten, and repurposed it as a fire-making device.

Nick appeared at the sliding-glass door, and I waved for him to join me.

"Whatcha doin', buddy?" he asked as he stepped outside.

I didn't even look up. I was too close to success.

"C'mere," I said, waving him over again. "Watch this."

I'd focused the sun's energy through the magnifying glass into a gorgeous, glowing white circle of pure light on the farthest left match tip in the book. I'd been hunched in this position for about a minute. The hand gripping the glass trembled, so I grabbed my wrist with the other hand to steady it.

A wire of smoke quickly rose from the red match head into the air.

Nick knelt beside me and curiously leaned in.

A bright spark!

The sharp yet intoxicating stink of sulfur!

A star-shaped burst of light and then the whole row of matches went up in beautiful flame!

I looked up at Nick with a proud grin.

He didn't seem nearly as impressed but he smiled back.

"That's pretty neat," he said, and I believed he genuinely meant it. My heart swelled.

The flame that engulfed the matchbook fluttered and shrank as it ate the paltry meal of thin cardboard. That little show was over, so I reached between my feet and pulled out what I'd been purposely concealing.

A gray moth, about the size of a fifty-cent piece from wingtip to wingtip, flapped madly against the small block of wood it was attached to. I'd run a thumbtack through one of its wings and fastened it to the wood. Nick's smile faded.

"What's that?" he asked.

"It's a moth, dummy," I said, brushing the smoldering matchbook aside. I put the wood block in its place.

"I see that, Daniel. What are you gonna do with it?"

"Watch."

Holding up the magnifying glass, I caught the sun and that same brilliant circle of light appeared on the moth's back. It was still for a second, no doubt exhausted from thrashing its body against the block in a hopeless attempt to escape, but when it felt that circle of heat, it commenced its panicky fluttering.

"Dan..."

I focused the circle into a pinpoint, concentrating the sun's energy into a direct laser.

"Dude, that's cruel," said Nick reproachfully.

"It's a moth, Nick. This is science."

There was a soft *thaap-thaap-thaap* as the moth attempted its getaway, beating its free wing and velvety thorax against the wood.

"Cut it out, Daniel."

"Just watch, this is gonna be cool."

"I don't think setting innocent creatures on fire and watching them burn alive is cool, Dan."

"Listen to yourself, pussy! It's just a moth!"

"Giving a shit about that moth does not make me a pussy."

"Well, why don't you call the PETA police, I'm sure they'll rush right over to save a moth. Oooh, it's starting to smoke!"

A thin tendril of black smoke rose from the moth's furry body.

And without further conversation, Nick reached out and plucked the thumbtack from the moth's wing. For an instant it was motionless, perhaps in shock from the pain, or it was simply admitting defeat. But then it beat both its wings against the wood block, and in three quick little bounces, fell off onto the patio. I flashed Nick a look of betrayal, but he was fixed on the flopping moth doing its best to take to the air, or at least to find cover, and so did not see my vexation.

When his eyes finally did meet mine, the look in them stung my heart in a way I'd never felt before. It was a look I'd seen dozens of times from Mom and Dad, but never a friend, certainly not one as close as Nick. Up until that moment, I'd never felt such a true sense of loneliness, which I thought odd because I certainly wasn't alone. I was with Nick. How could I feel so alone?

But it was in his eyes. Whatever came through Nick's eyes made me feel like I'd lost every person who'd ever cared for me.

Which made me angry.

"What the hell, man?" I said, my hackles raised.

"What?" said Nick, pretending like he didn't know why I was mad.

"You fucked up my experiment. I was showing you something cool."

"I didn't think it was cool, Dan, I thought I made that pretty clear."

"You didn't even wait to see what would happen, you missed the cool part!"

Nick stood. "We're gonna be late for the movie. Let's go."

"I don't wanna go," I said. The words exited my mouth and I immediately regretted saying them because *of course* I wanted to go, but pride is weird like that, isn't it? And once I'd said them, something in me was convinced I now had to defend those words like my life depended on it.

"Are you serious? Because I ruined your dumb little execution-by-fire?"

"Yes, I'm serious. It was rude and it was *my* experiment and you fucked it up and now I'm not in the mood."

"You sound like your parents."

"Fuck you."

I could tell that did something. Nick paused, eyebrows raised, searching my face to make sure I wasn't joking around, pulling his leg. When he found no humor in my expression, his face relaxed.

"Fine." He shook his head in disbelief. "Go burn all the moths you want."

He turned and left me in the backyard by myself.

The next day we made up and buried the hatchet, but it wasn't easy. I texted him *How was the movie* and he responded fairly quickly with *Awesome, you missed out*. I apologized for being a dickhead and he accepted and we moved on almost like nothing had happened.

Almost.

Truffles noticed I was lost in sad memories and changed the subject.

"There's a girl."

"Huh?"

"A girl. Back at school. We met in fencing class."

I smiled. "She likes you?"

"Yeah, I think. We've eaten lunch together a couple times. Her name is Piper."

"I like that name."

"She's a Theater major. I went to one of her plays. She's actually pretty good."

"That's cool, Truff, I'm happy for you."

"She says I remind her of a cuter Seth Rogan."

I laughed and pretended to size him up. "Yeah, I guess I can see that. Not cuter by much."

"Shut up, dickhole."

"I'm kidding, Truff, you're a catch."

"Don't patronize me."

"I'm serious. You're a catch. And Piper knows it."

If the biting air hadn't already turned Truffles' cheeks into ripe tomatoes I would have seen him blush. He grinned, embarrassed.

A full minute went by with us in silence. Dad, Henry, and Bert continued to talk in low voices.

I turned back to Truffles. With genuine perplexity I asked, "You're taking a fencing class?"

And right then, from inside the house, Chloe began to bark. All at once our heads turned, eyes on the sliding glass door. Neither Mom nor Chloe was in view. The barking I recognized immediately as Chloe's rapid-fire *There's-someone-at-the-door-and-I'm-not-okay-with-it* bark. Like when the UPS guy would drop off a package, or Jehovah's Witnesses would come to enlighten us.

"Well, sump'n pissed *her* off," said Bert.

I looked at Dad. He met my eyes right away.

There was no hesitation. Dad offered the rope to me.

At a run, he started up the backyard toward the house. Not three seconds later, Mom appeared behind the sliding glass door, her eyes unmistakably filled with an urgency that chilled me beyond the penetrating cold. She rapped very quietly on the glass of the door with one knuckle. Dad stopped in his tracks.

She pointed up.

We wouldn't know what was happening in the house until later, when Mom recounted to us what she saw...

Mom had been watching us the whole time from her bedroom window. She'd turned off all the lights just like Dad had commanded, but mostly to conceal her spying. She didn't quite understand what was going on, but all the same, her stomach was in knots and her heart pounded in her ears. She nervously picked at her cuticles, something she often did when she was on edge. Her eyes kept flicking to the neighbors' backyards, to Juniper's field, to the snow-covered maple trees lit by streetlights in the far distance, scanning for movement.

Chloe was on the bed resting her head calmly on her paws. She watched Mom watching us with mild curiosity. There was an uneasiness to her mistress but nothing to raise her hackles at, though she was certainly prepared to spring into action were the moment to require it. Thirty-eight minutes in, after watching her mistress take one bathroom break, shoot off a couple quick texts to Soren and Lilly, and fetch a glass of water, Chloe finally felt the need to spring.

The abrupt jingling of her dog tags, the way they broke the silence into a million glassy pieces, and then Chloe's subsequent launch from the bed, leaving the comforter a rumpled mess, put Mom's heart in her throat. She gasped and covered her mouth like some silly horror movie ingénue, blushing in spite of herself.

"Hey," she called after her dog, following her out of the bedroom.

Mom found Chloe at the living room window, standing on her hind legs with her front paws on the windowsill, a low growl rumbling in her throat. Her wet nose was pressed up against the glass.

"Chloe, get down," said Mom, pulling her away from the window. Her claws dug into the sill and left white marks in the brown paint. "What do you see, girl?"

Chloe obeyed her mistress but did not cease her growling. In fact, it seemed to ramp up a little, becoming shaky and almost crazed. Mom followed the dog's intense stare out the front window and realized whatever it was that had Chloe on the defensive (nay, had her coming unhinged) seemed to be on the rooftop of the neighbor's house across the street.

Mom leaned toward the glass, her eyes straining. The moonlight was dim but still cast a shadow of the chimney across the shingles of the roof. The streetlight several yards away did very little to illuminate the dark places Mom wanted to see into the most.

And then smoke appeared to be rising from the chimney. Impossible. Those neighbors were out of town. But there it was. A translucent, black vapor coming out of the smokestack.

Even through the darkness Mom could see the wispy fumes outlined against the night sky. Her first fear was that something had caught fire and was threatening to burn the house down, and then she feared someone had broken in and had lit up the flue. Neither scenario made much sense, and both were thrown out the window when the rising smoke fell back into the chimney, as if she were watching a movie and someone had just hit the rewind button for an instant replay. The smoke was gone but something had taken its place.

Mom stared in rapt fascination. There was now a mound, like the top of a head, barely peeking out from behind the top of the smokestack. Mom's heart rate picked up speed. Her breath fogged the glass. Chloe continued to growl, and from the sounds of it, Mom knew at any second Chloe was likely to lose her mind.

When a dark, upright figure stepped out from behind the neighbor's chimney, moonlight highlighting its inhuman contours, its hollow face turned in their direction, Mom screamed and Chloe lost it (from outside, all we heard was Chloe—that bitch is *loud*). By the time the air had left Mom's lungs, the *it* had crawled down the rooftop toward the ground and was launching itself to land in the snow. It moved with the speed and agility of a large cat, with the predatory determination to match.

Mom's limbs didn't immediately respond to the commands her brain was giving them and instead hung limply and trembled while she watched in terror as the monster (Mom's specific word for it) sprinted on four legs (legs?) across the snowy street and straight at the window through which Mom was looking. While Chloe continued to lose her shit, Mom's legs finally sprang into action like some Frankenstein lightning bolt had shocked them to life, and moved clear of the window. Her fingers fumbled for the drawstring of the curtain, found purchase, and yanked down hard. In one swift pull, the curtains closed over the window, concealing the house interior at the same time the monster collided with the glass.

But it wasn't a collision as if the monster had been trying to get inside. There were two squeaks of bare wet flesh against glass and then a sudden *gaTHUMP* on the roof. Both Mom and Chloe followed the sounds of clawed feet as they traveled across the rooftop, their noses pointed at the ceiling, Chloe's hysterical barking making the situation all the more terrifying. One singular thought swam to the surface of Mom's fear-clouded mind, and she knew she had to move fast —*It's coming right for them.*

I watched Mom's pointer finger eagerly directing my attention upward, and absurdly, the phrase *We're number one!* popped into my brain, but since that made next to no sense whatsoever, I decided to look up.

It wasn't there, and then it was, like a lightning flash or a car collision. It moved with such fluid grace that it was as beautiful as it was repulsive and I stared dumbly, unable to react, as it slithered down the shingles toward the eaves. *Like a snake with claws.*

"Heads up," Dad said, monotone. He backed away and we traded positions at the rope, me scampering back to the grill.

The low chitchat of the men abruptly ceased.

I heard Bert's voice: "Holy God."

The black creature, smaller now since Brett had bisected it with a snow shovel, took to the air and drifted to the snow-covered ground like a sugar glider, but far less adorable. It landed not two feet away from me. Those strange hollow eyes fixed on me and whatever heat I'd had left in my blood was immediately chilled.

It knows me.

I'm dead.

It dipped its head down, made contact with the snow, and then took a step toward me. I could see two egg-shaped holes in its face twitching.

It was smelling me.

The darkness seemed to gather around me like being at the bottom of a trash bag with the drawstrings pulling closed.

The thing's eyes narrowed as it studied me, and for the first time I could see a spark of intelligence. I would lie awake some nights in the aftermath of these events and wonder what role it played wherever it came from: was it animal, or something closer to human? Maybe something in between. Maybe neither.

It was starting to evaporate so it dipped its head into the snow again and then its elbows and fingers. And then, it turned to the fire. Its eyes widened and then relaxed, like it was at once reminded of why it had come and then was suddenly drugged. It crept cautiously forward but didn't seem to notice the four other men standing around the trap. For a half second, I thought I was alone, that everyone had fled the scene in fear and that I was left to spring the trap myself. But they were all in position: Dad and Bert behind the trailer, Truffles and Henry behind the swinging doors. And there were Truffles' legs sticking out of the bottom of the entry door. He poked his head out and quickly retracted it like a kid playing hide-and-seek. I realized I'd been holding my breath and released it in a slow, thick cloud.

Time stopped in the backyard as the inky creature made its way to the barbeque grill. I couldn't tell if the thing was crawling or floating, and again, the unnatural fluidity with which it moved struck me with horror. Where before at the Tomlinsons' the thing had been more curious about the fire, it now appeared covetous and wrapped itself around the grill like a dog protecting its food bowl. It still danced with the flickering flames, two lovers entwined, but occasionally stopped to worship. I couldn't help but be reminded of Gollum tenderly stroking that cursed ring.

Or of myself, for that matter. Firebug.

I shifted my gaze to behind the trailer, caught Dad's eye. I gave him the most imperceptible nod, thinking anything more would draw the creature's attention, and he returned the same. Very slowly, he crouched down and disappeared from sight again, and then the grill took its first inch forward.

The creature lurched back, not expecting it's *precious* to move away. It gave a canine head-tilt and then closed the gap, once again cradling the flames in its spindly arms. The grill continued to roll bit by bit across the platform, and our mouse continued to take the bait. My stomach dropped to my toes, however, when the wheels hit the lip of the ramp and stopped. The rope slacked, went taut, slacked, went taut as Dad carefully tried to ease the grill onto the ramp. It tilted back and forth like a rocking chair on fire. And as if that challenge weren't enough, said fire was starting to lose its height and girth. It was possible some of the kindling had gotten wet and wasn't going to burn correctly (*Fuck*). The grill teetered far forward, and I was certain it was about to tip, spilling charred wood and sparks and flames everywhere (*Fuck fuck*). Dad tried a different strategy and pulled the rope ever so slowly, and again I was sure the grill would tip, but the wheels cooperated and rolled gently over the lip and onto the ramp. Our mouse was right there with it. And it was right about then tough ol' cowboy Bert started acting squirrelly.

Much like Mom's perspective on the night would not be known until after the fact, so too would I later learn about the events leading up to Henry getting half of his left hand blown off.

Dad said from the moment Bert laid eyes on the *it*, there was an obvious shift in his behavior. The first thing he noticed was his breathing. It went from steady, calm, and uniform inhalations to uneven staccato breaths that never seemed to fill his lungs. Dad could barely take his own eyes off the black entity long enough to notice Bert's face, but if he had, he'd have surely seen a man drained of blood and suddenly come-to-Jesus (or rather, the other guy). No doubt the concept of an otherworldly being is dramatically different than the stark reality of it, and Bert Wickstrom was not faring well inside this new reality.

By the time Dad was reeling the flaming grill into the trailer he noticed Bert's calloused, wrinkled, and trembling left-hand fingers tickle at the holstered revolver. Though Bert was right-handed, his lack of an index finger on that hand made it difficult to pull a trigger. He'd clearly learned to shoot with his left, so wore the gun on the corresponding hip. Fucking *hope* he learned...if the random bullet-holes in the trailer were any indication of his marksmanship...

"Bert," Dad whispered, and tried shifting Bert's attention to the garden shears. Bert, his focus pointed through the small back window at the *it* drawing nearer, looked at my father as if he'd forgotten his name.

"The shears, Bert."

Bert neither responded nor even reacted to the urgency in Dad's tone. His right eye twitched and his left hand wrapped around the revolver's grip. Very slowly, as if he were hunting wild game, Bert withdrew the gun from its holster without making a sound.

"Bert," Dad whispered. "Stop."

From my vantage point, I could hear something wrong in Dad's voice but dared not move for fear I might spook the *it* and send it fleeing into the night. I did notice, however, the pace at which the grill was being pulled increased, and in two seconds, it disappeared inside the trailer.

Dad reached for the shears himself while also still reeling in our mouse. Bert, his upper lip curling into a sneer, raised the revolver.

The next string of events happened so quickly I barely had time to register if our trap worked or not.

"Bert, dammit," Dad hissed as he grabbed the shears with his left hand, the rope still in his right. But leaning over caused a sudden jerk in the tension and the silent night was jarringly broken by the metallic crash of the grill toppling to the trailer floor.

Henry and Truffles followed through with their parts, lifting the ramp and swinging the trailer doors to close. Before they could be secured, the revolver exploded with a shot that rang loudly inside the metal cage, bleeding into Henry's unexpected screaming. I watched, momentarily stunned as Truffles threw the lock on the doors and Henry staggered out from behind the trailer, his left hand inside a red glove.

"GodfuckingChrist!" he yelled, staring at the spot where two fingers used to be.

"Daniel!" Dad hollered.

I wheeled around the trailer to see Dad shoving Bert out of the way, the old man stumbling backward in the snow. Dad was attempting to clip the rope with the shears himself. The fibers made a grinding, ripping sound as they split apart.

"Grab the plank!"

As I did, I caught a glimpse of our mouse. It was panicked, and moving toward us like a disturbed spider, hoping to escape out the window. The spilt grill behind it was no longer of any interest even though the wood still burned and the embers popped.

The rope snapped and Dad flung the frayed end attached to the grill inside the trailer.

"Cover the window NOW!"

The plank collided with the creature and the force of it sent me backwards. "Truffles!"

I quickly recovered and thrust the plank over the open window again. A spine-chilling wail issued from the inside of the trailer. Opposing pressure hammered against the plank. Dad grabbed the screw gun, his gloved fingers fumbling with the screws. Truffles rounded the corner as shiny, black tentacles like those of a squid began seeping out from behind the plank.

"Dad—" I pushed against the force of *it* as hard as I could. Truffles came to my aid as Dad ripped his gloves off with his teeth. Fingers freed, he stabbed the first screw into the corner of the plank. Truffles was putting everything he had into keeping that window covered; it was like trying to shut a door against hurricane-force winds. The wailing was growing in pitch, becoming a full-fledged scream as the glossy tendrils searched for purchase, flailing like eels caught in a net.

Dad started that first screw, throwing an elbow against the plank for added resistance. The scream rose to a crescendo and split into what sounded like several painful roars as we pushed against the plank. For an instant I had a terrifying thought (*My name is Legion, for we are many*) that the *it* had somehow duplicated itself innumerably, and at any moment Hell was going to break free from our feeble, man-made, hubristic mousetrap. Instead, the black tentacles severed under the force of our strength like fingers in a guillotine and fell limply to the ground.

One screw secured.

Two screws.

Dad moved with a swiftness that defied his age and the numbing cold. The legion of roars continued (a petrifying sound that would haunt our nights for the next four days) and a violent series of metallic crashes shook the trailer as the creature within frenziedly tried to escape.

Three screws. Four.

The grimace of putting forth his greatest effort didn't leave Truffles' face. I imagined mine looked similar. We pushed and pushed despite losing our balance once or twice beneath the abrupt rocking of the trailer.

Five screws. Six. Seven. Eight.

I glanced toward the house and saw Mom rushing out with a dishtowel and Henry stumbling to meet her. I think Mom was saying something, but it was indiscernible. She cradled Henry's hand within the towel and hurried him inside. The faintest scent of gathering wood smoke touched my nostrils.

Nine screws.

I turned my eyes to Dad. The screw gun *yeeeeeeep'd* as it drove that tenth screw into the wood and metal. His tongue poked out the corner of his mouth, just like mine does when I'm concentrating. The screw gun fell quiet even though the night did not. He stopped, panting. The trailer continued to tremble as if we'd just caged a small rhinoceros. Dad raised the screw gun again.

Eleven. For good measure.

Dad circled the trailer, double-checking for holes, cracks, the slightest cranny through which a creature like ours could possibly escape, but everything seemed to check out. As far as he could tell, the trailer was secure and the mouse was trapped. And then he turned to Bert with that look, *the* look, the one I always feared growing up.

"What the hell happened, Bert?" His voice was low, his emotions controlled, but beneath the lid, bubbling fury.

Bert, who'd only been able to stand back and watch the plan carried out from feet away with a look of stupefaction, stared at my father with sudden contempt, as if Benjamin was the one to blame. "That...*thing*—"

"We had a plan, Bert, a goddamn plan. You could have killed someone."

"Don't you talk to me that way, Benny boy. This is *my* trailer, that thing killed *my* cows—"

"What were you thinking? After all the things my son told you about that thing, you still thought you could just *shoot* it for Christ's sake?"

Bert took a step closer to Dad as if tempting a duel. In

stature, Bert paled in comparison, but even cocker spaniels think they can threaten rottweilers.

"Now you listen to me. Ain't nobody never seen nothin' like this before so nobody's no expert on how to kill it."

"But the plan was never to kill it, Bert, the plan was to trap it."

"Didn't you see the way he was comin' at us? It was either him or us."

Dad took a deep breath in an effort to calm down.

"I'm not really the one you should be explaining to. I don't know the extent of his injuries, but you'll be lucky if Henry ever forgives you. Hell, he may even press charges. Desmond, too."

Truffles flinched. Both Dad and I looked at him expectantly but all he could do was blush.

"Let's get inside, boys," said Dad to Truffles and me, patting my shoulder and turning toward the house.

We left Bert, angry and speechless, his pistol still in his grip but now hanging flaccidly at his side. Truffles tromped a few steps behind Dad and me. And only Bert and I caught the single-most rebellious thing Truffles ever did on his own, and I loved him all the more for it; after all, that bullet just as easily could have gone straight through Truffles' brain as it had gone through Henry's hand.

Chin up and eyes narrowed, Truffles extended his middle finger and flipped Bert right the fuck off.

Mom already had her coat, scarf, and gloves on in preparation to drive Henry to the hospital when we came through the sliding-glass door. Henry stood over the kitchen sink, his hand wrapped in the blood-saturated dishtowel. A tiny crimson bulb was forming at the bottom of it, quivering.

"Christ, Henry," started Dad, "I don't know what the hell happened—"

"We can talk later, Ben," Mom cut in, pulling a navy-blue stocking cap over her ears. "I'm taking him to the ER."

"I'm going with you," he said without hesitation.

"Grab another dishtowel, will you? That one's soaked through."

Dad opened a kitchen drawer and pulled out the first thing he came to: a white-and-red towel with Santa and his eight tiny reindeer soaring in silhouette against a yellow moon. Henry dropped the blood-soaked towel into the sink and for a couple seconds, we all got a look at the damage.

There was nothing left of Henry's pinkie and ring fingers except two gory nubs. The ragged flesh looked angry and almost black, and there was a tiny glint of bone peeking out. I wondered if he was left- or right-handed and what difference this handicap would make in his future. Hopefully he was right-handed and the difference wouldn't be much. But still... those were his damn fingers. Bert had no right to take those away, accident or not. The strange sense of irony or coincidence or whatever was not lost on me.

Henry's pallor was ashy and he looked on the verge of fainting as Dad wrapped the Santa Claus dishtowel around his dripping hand.

"It's gonna be alright, Henry, just hang in," he said in a low voice.

Henry chuckled. "Aw, the hell it is."

"Good news is, we got it. Captured and secured."

"Figured. I can hear it carrying on out there."

Mom waved her arms in a *get going* gesture. "All right fellas, load into the car, let's move." She sounded like a military general ordering her platoon.

The patio door slid open and in walked the cowboy with the itchy trigger finger. Mom's head snapped around so fast I thought it would break her neck. There was fire in her eyes. She thrust one threatening finger at the pistol now holstered at Bert's waist.

"I want that *thing* out of my house immediately, Bert Wickstrom, and God help you if I ever see it again."

She didn't wait for a response, but shuffled the men out the door and into the garage. "Daniel, keep your cell on, I'll call when we get to the hospital."

The three of us, Truffles, Bert, and myself, were left there, standing awkwardly in the kitchen without much to say even though so much had just happened. In the background, the *it* bellowed and thrashed against the trailer. The moment would have been almost comical if it wasn't so nerve-wracking.

Finally, Truffles broke the uneasiness. "Do you think its gonna do that all night?" he asked.

I shrugged. "I don't know, Truff."

Bert punctuated the moment by clearing his throat and showing himself to the door. Without a word, he unceremoniously left the house, gently closing the door behind him. A wave of relief washed over me. But in a way, I felt sort of bad for the guy. A person knows when they've done wrong. Sure, the gun should never have come into play, but when fear, fear the likes of which you've never known before, grips you and takes control, who among us can say beyond the shadow of a doubt how they would respond? Bert, in his limited world views and perhaps below-average intelligence, responded the only way he knew how. It was the response equal to the sum of his parts.

But still, he shot Henry's fucking hand off.

By bringing the gun, he made a choice, neither good nor bad.

He just took it too far.

Truffles left shortly afterward, and I assured him I'd keep him in the loop regarding our little fire-loving prisoner. When Mom called, all the militancy was gone from her voice and had been replaced with calm concern. I told her I was fine, there is nothing to worry about here, how is Henry, and are they going to give him robot fingers. She sighed and chuckled and said the doctors stopped the bleeding but robot fingers are still in question.

I lay on my bed above the covers in the dark, listening to the screeching sounds from the trailer gradually dying down (the creature no doubt on the brink of complete exhaustion) and wondered when those neighbors who hadn't left town for the holidays would ask questions. And what we would tell them. And lamented the fact we didn't get to celebrate the success of our mousetrap due to blown-off fingers and an ER trip. But maybe that was good. Maybe that was right. Maybe it didn't deserve celebrating. As my drained body and weary mind began to wander toward the Land of Nod I had one final, lucid thought: *You're a firebug, too.*

Sleep took me before Mom and Dad returned home from the ER and kept me until well into midmorning the next day.

CHAPTER SEVEN

Christmas Eve traditions in our household are always strictly enforced by Soren. It's the one day out of the entire year when he actually seems to give a shit about being together as a family and doing special things as a group. It started before Mom and Dad's separation, but it wasn't until after they got back together that he took on a sort of totalitarian rule over the events of Christmas Eve. We figured it was his strange way of ensuring the family remained together this time, and no one ever really balked at him. In fact, Lilly was beginning to take up his mantle and was becoming just as whiny if things didn't go according to the traditional schedule.

Which was as follows:

Mom makes breakfast (silver dollar pancakes, sausage links *not* patties, cream cheese scrambled eggs, fresh-squeezed orange juice [and for the *fresh-squeezed* part, Soren was a particular sort of Nazi] and tiny blueberry muffins), followed by the Sibling Snowball Fight (which was usually me against Soren and Lilly—the eldest has an advantage and has to roll solo apparently--I never minded), and while this is going on,

Mom and Dad enjoy the remainder of the orange juice but spike it with champagne and sit in front of the fire for some alone time while reminiscing about Christmases past or whatever (I don't really want to think about the "whatever").

Then showers, we get dressed, and pile into the car for last minute Christmas shopping. Since there's one department store in Ferdinand, it shouldn't take nearly as long as it does. But it's fun and there's secrets and alliances and *No peeking* and good-natured family feuding while Christmas music plays in the background and fellow shoppers with easy smiles pass and say "Merry Christmas" and lights twinkle and chintzy decorations reflect the season and an otherwise typical trip to the store becomes something more.

Then it's back home to wrap those gifts in secret while Mom and Dad sip eggnog and Chloe barks for attention. Its right about then that Dad starts dinner (homemade spaghetti with a pork sausage red sauce [*never* ground beef on Christmas Eve] and the longest loaf of garlic bread you've ever laid your eyes on), with Dad making the same joke he does every year: "So this is enough for me, I don't know what *you're* all gonna eat!" and Soren and Lilly laugh and Mom and I roll our eyes but smile too. Before Grandma and Grandpa died (Mom's folks) they'd arrive for a cocktail and dinner and deliver their gifts to us kids. They both passed in 2014 but we always honor their memory when we go around the table to express our individual gratitudes.

We eat, we chat, we laugh and fight and most times Mom cries and then us kids do the dishes while Mom and Dad pick out the one gift we get to open before Christmas morning. They turn on the Christmas music (usually John Denver and the Muppets or Kenny Rogers and Dolly Parton) and they carefully sift through the presents beneath the Christmas tree, searching for the one special gift for each of us, the one that simply can't wait until morning. Then they pick one for each other as well, and once the dishes are done and put away, we all gather around the tree and sit in a circle (with Chloe too) and we open our gifts, oldest to youngest, so by the time it reaches Soren and Lilly they're both practically clawing at the paper and ravenous for what's underneath it. It's rarely a disappointment, and the evening of tradition continues with the annual viewing of *Home Alone*. If everyone is still wide-awake by the time the credits roll, *National Lampoon's Christmas Vacation* goes into the DVD player. Most years, the kids don't make it past that one. They're off to bed where visions of sugarplums can dance in their heads, and Mom, Dad, and I play Santa and prepare Soren and Lilly's bounty from jolly ol' Saint Nick. The year we had to put together the Foosball table is still my favorite; I'm not sure I've ever laughed so hard in my life.

After that, I usually shove off to bed myself, but the last few years, the three of us have begun a new tradition. We throw on *It's a Wonderful Life* and just chat. We chat about school, work, music, anything. I let them ask me questions about girls, and they answer questions about adulthood. Some of the most earnest moments with my parents *together* have been late night Christmas Eves.

This year, however, a wrench was thrown in the usual day of tradition; a wrench in the form of whatever it was caged in the trailer in the backyard.

As the silver dollar pancakes bubbled on the skillet, Mom said no Sibling Snowball Fight this year, not if we planned on staging it in the backyard (which we always did—our backyard was huge and there were lots of places to take cover), to which Soren replied with his most sulky, me-against-the-world spew of teenage angst: "How can you do this, Dad said that thing is locked up tight, there's no danger, you're being unreasonable, you're ruining Christmas, look at Lilly's face, she's about to cry, etc, etc." Mom, never one to negotiate with terrorists but knowing how much this day meant to Soren, softened a touch and got ample reassurance from Dad.

"It's okay, love. That thing isn't going anywhere. Just…stay away from the trailer, okay kids? Don't do anything to… provoke it."

So, after breakfast, we geared up in our winter clothes and set out to battle. The trailer at the far end of the yard had gone silent and still, which was a marked change from the early morning hours when its occupant had set about trying to wake every sleeping man, woman, and child within a fifty-mile radius. The howling sent chills through me, and all I could think of was how lucky we were most of our neighbors were out of town for the holidays. That, and *I wonder what its thinking?*

The rules were simple: we had ten minutes to make as many snowballs as we could and pick our "home base" for snowball storage. Once those snowballs were gone, you could make three more on the fly before the game was over. Each team was responsible for keeping track of how many personal hits the other got. The one with the most hits won. There have only been two years in the history of this tradition where I haven't won. Just sayin'.

The sky was cloudless and crystal blue, the sun reflecting off the snow with blinding intensity. Soren, practically twitching with bloodlust, hurled the first snowball and missed hitting my left arm by a hair. I countered and also missed but nailed the naked apple tree. A white lump stuck to the trunk. Lilly threw next and I didn't duck behind the corner of the house quick enough and she got me in the belly.

"Direct hit!" squealed Soren gleefully. He and Lilly did a happy dance. And in their hubris, they were both struck in the face by my patented Double Throw of Death. Lilly laughed, shaking snow out of her hair, and bent down behind the woodpile that served as their home base and armed herself with another snowball. Soren scowled at me from across the yard, his cheeks wet with melting snow, and I knew his vengeance would be swift and vicious.

But he never got to retaliate because right then the *it* woke up.

Lilly's giggles were interrupted with a mournful wail so haunting it made every hair on my body stand on end. It was oddly prehistoric, like you would never hear such a sound while humans roamed the earth. That cry was meant for the end of things. It was loneliness and despair and anger expressed in one singular sound.

We all stood erect, our heads turned toward the trailer, hearts pounding. A diamond of sunlight reflected off the curved corner of the metal. We didn't move, *couldn't* move, as the wail tapered off and then stopped. At last, Soren spoke.

"I want to see it."

"No."

"It's not fair Mom shipped us out to friends' houses last night. You guys all got to see it."

Lilly chimed in. "I didn't see it. I don't want to see it."

"You're not seeing it, Soren. There aren't any peepholes or

anything anyway, we sealed them all up. C'mon, let's take this to the front yard."

Soren took a few steps toward the trailer. Inside, the creature was chittering, mumbling. The sounds were soft, like it was talking to itself. It was almost cute.

"Just let me try…" he said.

"Soren," started Lilly, catching up to him, "if you go near that trailer, I'll tell Mom and Dad and they'll kick your butt."

"Dammit, Soren, stop," I hissed. "Just leave it alone!"

Soren ignored us and crept right up to the shiny metal. He searched with his fingers for any rust-eaten hole or crack, but they'd all been caulked, sealed, and boarded. The chittering stopped and I held my breath. Soren pressed his ear against the metal.

"Hello in there," he said whimsically, like he was speaking to a small child playing hide-and-seek. "What are you doing in there?"

The slam came hard and fast and I nearly jumped right out of my snow boots. Soren fell backward, arms pinwheeling, and landed in the snow looking like he was preparing to make a snow angel. The force of the hit tilted the trailer at a forty-five-degree angle, and there it teetered on two wheels.

This is it. This is how my brother dies. Crushed beneath a—

And then my legs kicked in and I was sprinting across the yard, throwing up great sprays of powder.

The trailer moaned under rusty axles as it swayed, suspended in the air waiting to deliver Soren's judgment. As I reached him, sliding into home plate, the die was cast, and it was decided Soren would live. The trailer tipped the other direction and, with a springy *crunch*, righted itself.

Breathless, we stared at the trailer, waiting for something

to happen. Lilly plopped herself down with us in the snow, and if Mom and Dad had looked out the window in that moment, they would have chewed all our asses.

Inside, the trailer had fallen silent once more.

I patted a gloved hand on Soren's heaving chest. "We're done here."

He nodded.

"Yeah."

None of us mentioned Soren's little stunt to Mom and Dad, and the day carried on like it always did. At the department store, Soren was a little less jovial than he was most years, perhaps because he was still contemplating the possibility of his untimely death. I teased him while in the books and magazines aisle if he'd seen his pathetic life flash before his eyes, filled with nothing but snippets of him jerking off and playing video games. He said no, there were flashes of pizza and sleeping till noon, too. We both smiled and I slapped his back and headed off to find Lilly in the toy department. That was as close to a hug as we would get.

The rest of Christmas Eve went mostly according to Soren's plan. Dad made spaghetti with pork sausage, we each opened one gift (I was pretty pleased to get a package of new guitar strings), and then we sat down to watch *Home Alone*. Chiefly, the one difference was the apocalyptic wail coming from the backyard. It mixed with the scene where Kevin McCallister is looking forlornly at a framed picture of his family and regretting making them disappear, and it pulled at my heartstrings in a way it never had before. *He's lonely. Yeah, he originally wanted his family to go away but now he sees the error of his ways and just wants them back.*

Ugh, shut up, Dan.

That thing…must be lonely too.

Shut UP, it eats babies! Babies, Dan!

Both Soren and Lilly were fast asleep in the blanket nest they'd made on the floor by the time the McCallisters were reunited. Mom escorted them both to bed to ensure neither one would sneak out and spy us playing Santa. Soren, of course, knew it was us, but the magic still existed for Lilly. I wondered how many more years she'd believe. No doubt her friends at school were already questioning the fat guy in the red suit and perhaps putting seeds of suspicion in her eight-year-old brain. For her sake (and maybe mine too), I hoped she believed for a few more years.

We skipped *National Lampoon's Christmas Vacation* and went right to *It's a Wonderful Life* after setting out Santa's offerings. And the whole time, we could hear our mouse in the trailer.

Mom and Dad sat next to each other on the couch and she suddenly gripped Dad's arm with a claw.

"Are you sure, Ben, absolutely sure there's nothing else to be done about that *thing*? It's making me crazy."

Dad's jaw clenched. "We stick to the plan. We wait, starve it out."

Mom, clearly not satisfied with this answer, released a great sigh that had so much subtext it was almost hard not to laugh. She could see the resolve in Dad's face. After a few seconds, and more to himself than to her, he said, "We stick to the plan."

That night my sleep was fraught with nightmares and they were far from the sugarplums and reindeer and Santa squeezing his fat ass down the chimney that they were allegedly supposed to be. But given the past few weeks, I could hardly blame my brain for needing to dump some of the horror it had accumulated.

There was one particular dream that woke me from sleep in a cold sweat. It was one of those dreams where you're both the observer (in this case, I was my little sister Lilly) and the one observing the observer. It's like being the main character in a movie while simultaneously sitting in the audience and watching the movie. It would toggle back and forth where one minute I was looking through Lilly's eyes and experiencing things *as her*, and the next, I was this omniscient onlooker.

The dream starts in my (Lilly's) bedroom. There is a clatter on the rooftop that shakes me from slumber. I hold my breath, awaiting another sound.

There it is again!

Like someone in thick-soled boots dancing around...

Or hooves!

I clutch the hem of my comforter and pull it up around my face, my eyes barely peeking out.

Is that bells?

Did I just hear the sound of bells?

I hold my breath and listen closely, ears straining.

A shaft of brilliant moonlight streams through my window and lights my door, as if not merely suggesting but insisting I go and open it.

Lilly throws off her covers. She is wearing a nightgown with Princess Elsa from *Frozen* printed on it. It is faded from being worn and washed too many times. She steps into that shaft of blue moonlight and reaches a tiny hand out to the doorknob.

Another clatter!

Perhaps Santa unloading his sack full of presents? Perhaps the reindeer stomping with impatient excitement?

I turn the doorknob and exit my room. The hallway is dark and I can hear the grandfather clock ticking. I didn't know we had a grandfather clock, but there it is, tick-tick-ticking away the seconds. I tiptoe past Mom and Dad's room, past Dan's and Soren's rooms, and make my way to the staircase. Downstairs is where the Christmas tree is. And the fireplace (Our actual house was only one-story but in this version, we had a two-story and it didn't seem odd. That's dream-logic for you).

Another clatter! But more like a scratching sound...a dragging sound...

Lilly stops in the middle of the stairs and looks up, her eyes following the direction of the sound.

It's Santa for sure!

Stepping extra lightly to not wake Mom or Dad, Lilly finishes her descent down the staircase. The Christmas tree glows with multicolored lights and there's a sort of halo around it, a natural rainbow corona. And just behind it is the fireplace. There is a stone hearth and there are five stockings hanging from the mantle above the crackling fire. The scene is picture-perfect, right out of a Christmas movie.

I take a step closer to the fireplace, my excitement mounting. A flurry of soot trickles down the chimney and into the fire. A sound of scratching against brick.

Here comes Santa Claus, Here comes Santa Claus...

I take a few steps closer. Oh man, this is the coolest thing to ever happen! I can't believe it! I'm gonna meet Santa!

Here comes Santa Claus, Here comes Santa Claus, right down Santa Claus Lane…

He better be careful, though, there's a fire in there. He's liable to burn his butt!

I laugh to myself at the thought of this.

Lilly pushes strands of her blonde hair behind her ears in preparation to meet the Big Guy. Her cheeks are flushed. Her eyes sparkle with firelight. A bird's-eye-view shows her tiny figure, the top of her small blonde head, edging past the Christmas tree and closer to the fireplace.

I wonder what he has for me! I asked for a new bike this year! One with glittery streamers that flow out of the handle-bars! And a princess dress! Like Elsa's!

The house falls silent as the grave. Even the fire seems to have lost its crackle. Or have I just tuned everything out? I'm close enough to the hearth to reach out and touch it. Something tells me this is close enough; I don't want to startle him when he makes his grand entrance. I can feel the air around me buzzing like a high-tension wire, and it seems to promise that something amazing is about to happen. A slight, cold draft exhales from the chimney and blows silky loose threads of my hair back. It carries with it a strange, unfamiliar smell. Not like soot and wood smoke. Like rotten eggs and fresh tar. Like bad memories and scary dreams. Like waking up with the flu at two a.m. and puking your guts out alone in a dark bathroom (But how can that have a *smell*? That's silly. But it does). Another rivulet of powdery soot cascades from the chimney and into the flames. And for the first time since getting out of bed, I feel afraid.

Scratch. Scratch.

I take one step back from the hearth.

Louder now. Closer. *Scratch, scratch.*

Here comes Santa Claus…

Two hands wearing shiny black leather gloves slowly sink down out of the chimney and into view. They search and wave like the tentacles of a sea anemone, curious and seductive.

Santa has really long fingers.

But those aren't fingers at all.

Those aren't hands wearing leather gloves.

Those are tendrils, like vines that climb up walls. Black vines.

Lilly takes another step back. The shiny black tentacles spread out from the fireplace. She counts eight, ten, *fifteen* of them! They slither outward, knocking a few of the stockings off their hooks. They reach up and grip onto the mantle. They flex, tighten, like an octopus preparing to drag its body forward.

I open my mouth to scream but nothing audible comes out, just raspy air. I try to run away but my feet are stuck in quicksand or tar even though I'm looking right at them and they're not stuck in anything! I close my eyes against this horror but my eyelids are see-through. There is no escaping this.

The tentacles start to go slack as they pull down the body of whatever it is coming into the house.

And that's when I realize: it's our mouse. It's the *it*. Somehow it found a way out of the trailer. And now it's come for me.

The thought is fleeting and quickly replaced with raw terror as the body emerges from the chimney. Two clawed hands drop onto the fire like twin jackhammers and sparks go flying. The charred wood splits under the force and chunks spin out of the fireplace and onto the carpet. A head emerges but it's mostly just a mouth, a mouth opened wide in a silent scream, and then a chest, a torso…black…shiny…like fresh tar…

The tentacles spread out, enveloping the room, like a spider casting filaments of web to encase its prey. A low branch on the Christmas tree tickles my bare calf and I turn to see there are six or seven black tendrils circling the decorated pine, hugging it and drawing it close as if it were a lover.

The *it* fully drops out of the chimney and lands on all fours. Its hind legs are hocked, like a wolf's or a panther's, and it begins to move toward her. The smoldering chunks of wood catch the carpet on fire and before Lilly knows it, the floor is burning from end to end.

It's like the real-life version of *the floor is lava* game.

"Mommy!" Lilly screams, momentarily shocked that her voice has returned. "Mommy, Daddy!" She screams loudly, louder than she ever has before. She tries to move her feet but they are still firmly fastened to the floor by invisible bonds. The fire is inches away from her. The heat is starting to burn her exposed skin. It feels like the worst sunburn of all time.

The creature floats down from the hearth in one graceful move and steps into the fire, unaffected. Its mouth is still screaming, and there are fangs in it, but not two fangs like a vampire—*all* the teeth are fangs, top row and bottom row, and they seem to be elongating with every passing second, spinning like sharp tornadoes.

The Christmas tree catches on fire. More tentacles are appearing—twenty, thirty, a hundred. The entire room from ceiling to floor is moving, *undulating* with black snakes. The walls are alive with them.

"Mommy! Daddy!"

Do they not hear me? Are they still fast asleep?

No, they're dead.

The thought comes aggressively, and I am certain they are dead. Upstairs, in their beds, looking as if they're sleeping but they're not. Dan and Soren too.

Tentacles are creeping beneath my feet now to the point where I can't even feel the carpet anymore. It feels like I'm standing on a tangle of writhing earthworms.

The fire draws closer, the fangs grow longer, and all at once, my *Frozen* nightgown is lit with flame and burns almost instantly off my body.

And then, I am both burning alive and being dined upon by the *it*. The pain is incomprehensible. The fear is mostly gone now, and I find myself yearning for the sweet release of death. Please take me away from this. Hurry and take me away.

Sweat. Blood. Flame.

And that's when I woke up gasping for breath, sitting bolt upright in bed, my sheet drenched. I could still feel my scorched skin tingling, my lungs burning with black smoke. I could feel the sting of a dozen fangs sinking into my face. Jesus Christ.

I grabbed my cell phone, checked the time: 3:55 a.m.

Just a dream. Just a fucked-up dream.

I lay my head back down and winced. With a flip of the pillow, my head found a dry surface.

It's trapped. It's not getting out.

It was an hour before I felt myself drifting back out to sea on a soft wave. The mournful keening from our mouse was the last thing I heard before sleep wrapped me in its dark cocoon, but it did not frighten me.

It's trapped. It's not getting out.

This time, against logic, the thought wrenched my heart.

Ferdinand awoke to a Christmas morning lost in a soupy fog, the kind where your neighbor's house, while merely across the street, is only an outline of where you thought a house once stood. It seemed a more appropriate aesthetic for Halloween than Christmas: ghostly and sinister, the mist more than likely concealing angry spirits jealously walking among the living. It was more Ebenezer Scrooge and his three fearsome ghosts than George Bailey and his wingless, bumbling angel. The sun wasn't even a barely glowing disc in the sky; the sun was altogether gone.

Outside, Ferdinand was haunted.

But inside, the joy and excitement of Christmas morning was alive and well, if only through Lilly's exuberant cheers and screams. I needed two cups of coffee in me to, at the very least, tolerate her squeals of delight. I did find it relieving to see her happy face after the nightmare I'd had of her close encounter with our mouse. For a few short minutes, the dream came back to me at full-force and I had to momentarily leave the room, but it dissipated like pipe smoke after a few deep breaths. After that second cup, Christmas would kick in, but until then, joy was hard to muster. Especially given the fitful night of sleep.

The caffeine from the first cup was doing its job nicely, and the second steaming cup was in my hands when Mom asked me to take Chloe out front for her morning pee. Since we'd parked the trap in the backyard and caged the *it*, Chloe refused to set a paw beyond the sliding-glass door. In fact, she spent most of her days inside, hiding in the corner of Lilly's bedroom between her bed and dresser. Whenever we took her out to do her business, she had to be leashed. We didn't quite yet trust her to stay put. And we couldn't exactly blame her. The very thing that had caused her to run away had now taken up residency in her territory. When Lilly would comfort the dog and then look accusingly at Dad as if it were somehow his fault, he would always say, "Hopefully this will be over soon," and then kind of drift away with a furrowed brow and hurt in his eyes.

"We stick to the plan. We wait, starve it out."

But how long is that gonna take, Pops? Nobody knows. It's still strong enough to nearly topple the trailer and it's still making plenty of noise at night. It seems very much alive still.

I leashed Chloe and slid on my jacket and boots and the two of us left the warm, sparkly glow of Christmas morning for the cold wasteland that our neighborhood had become.

The fog was so dense, so pervasive that I could literally feel it enter my lungs—cold and smothering—whenever I took a breath. Deciduous trees, barren of leaves, looked eerily like skeletons in the mist that would, at any moment, animate and chase unlucky passers-by through the nightmarish landscape. It was a world lost in white, from the ground to the sky. From across town, church bells rang out the tune to *Ave Maria*, determined to stir up feelings of Christmas despite the apocalyptic atmosphere. The beautiful simplicity of those bells caused a strange sadness to rise within me however, like this was the last Christmas the world would ever see again.

Though they tried to be a song of peace, for me, they sounded more like a requiem.

Chloe sniffed around on the snowy front lawn, and I let her drag me to the perfect place to pee. It was next to our ponderosa pine and a few feet from the sidewalk.

In mid-pee, Chloe's ears perked up. I heard it too. The *clip-clop* of thick-soled shoes walking down the street toward us.

Through the fog there was nothing, just sounds without an image, and although it was more than likely someone taking a Christmas stroll, I couldn't deny the rush of anxiety pounding through my chest. All I could think of was doomed Ichabod Crane riding horseback through Sleepy Hollow, and the headless menace stalking him.

Clip-clop. Clip-Clop.

Chloe, unable to see the approaching beings growled deep in her throat, her hackles raised, forming a ridge of fur down her spine. I rubbed her ears to calm her nerves. And mine.

In the white murk, two figures began taking shape, one smaller than the other. Slowly, there was a pair of broad shoulders, a dark coat; a graceful gait, shoulder-length auburn-colored hair beneath a hat with a fuzzy ball on top. A beard: epic.

And a face I wished many times in high school I could wake up next to.

Rebecca and Brett emerged from the wispy haze like time travelers entering an unfamiliar land when they spotted me. Right away I was glad to see them; after all, we'd shared an intimate supernatural experience and hadn't spoken about it since. I felt a strange sense of camaraderie when I finally recognized their faces through the fog, and I smiled with relief and took a step toward them even though Chloe was still growling.

"Hey," I said, and it came out froggy and muted. I cleared my throat and said it again. "Hey."

Without breaking stride, Rebecca flashed a quick grin and Brett threw an arm over her shoulder. Neither of them met my eyes for more than a second. Hardly the way you greet a neighbor or friend on Christmas morning. And certainly not how you greet someone you shared an intimate supernatural experience with. Right?

Rebecca managed a tiny "Hi," sans eye contact, as they *clip-clopped* on the shoveled sidewalk past Chloe and me. My sense of relief turned sour and my first cup of coffee surged bitterly up my esophagus, my stomach suddenly burning. I watched them disappear back into the mist, continuing on as if I were only a simple stranger they'd felt obligated to respond to and wanted to move past as quickly as possible.

"Merry Christmas," I called out after them, but not without a tiny trace of disdain. No response.

Ouch.

As they vanished behind the white veil my heart broke a little, and I was spitefully glad that Chloe's growling hadn't ceased as they'd walked by.

My thoughts ran rampant:

Why would they snub me like that? What did I do? Did I say something wrong? I basically saved them. Seriously, what the fuck? Maybe they're afraid of me. Yeah, they acted like they were afraid. But I'm not the monster—the thing in the backyard is the monster. I don't get it. I'm just Daniel. This is happening to me, I didn't cause this. Right? No, that's dumb. They should not have treated me that way. I'm never jerking off to her again. And his beard is fucking stupid. Okay, I might jerk off to her again.

"C'mon girl," I said to Chloe, pulling lightly on the leash.

Done with her business, and satisfied with having warded off that immediate threat, Chloe bounced ahead of me, ready to enjoy the comforts of a warm home with the rest of her pack, if only from the corner of Lilly's room.

The fog lingered most of the day and did not lift until right around dinnertime. Looking into the backyard through the sliding-glass doors and seeing the trailer obscured by the haze somehow made the creature within it more chilling. Random recurring flashes of my nightmare didn't help either. I wondered, as I had many times since caging it, what it was doing. What was it thinking? Did it know why it had become a prisoner? Did it have any clue about what was planned for it? That last question always bit at my heart.

It was during our very traditional Christmas dinner that Mom and Dad disclosed to Lilly and Soren that they should expect another sibling in about 8 months. I feigned surprise while Lilly squealed with glee at the prospect of getting a baby sister, and Soren was just more or less perplexed.

"How is that possible? You guys are so *old*."

"Well Soren, sweetie," started Mom politely, "a woman's reproductive system can still function into her forties."

"Eww, *stop!* Don't say reproductive system, I don't want to think about you two reproducing!"

Mom's eyes were silver dollars. "I don't want you to think about it either, Soren, *Jesus*."

"You do know that's how babies are made, right Soren?"

Dad asked. "Or do we need to have a talk with your Health teacher?"

After dinner, Lilly and Soren separated from the family to privately enjoy their Christmas gifts in their bedrooms. I helped Mom and Dad with the dishes and then retreated to my own room. I decided to restring my guitar, maybe pluck around for a bit, see if any inspiration would come to me. In the middle of tightening the fourth string, there was a knock on my cracked-open door.

"Hey son."

Dad waited for me to invite him in. He was looking a little worn out, and I couldn't say I blamed him. The past few days had been trying for both of us.

"Thought you might be interested to know how Henry is doing. Just got off the phone with his wife, she gave me an update."

I nodded, set my guitar aside.

"Josie said he's in surprisingly good spirits. There's some pain, and he's experiencing that whole phantom limb thing, but overall he seems to be adjusting relatively smoothly."

"That's good," I said. "I still can't believe Bert pulled that gun out. Piece of work. I wonder if he even feels bad."

"He'll wrestle with it for a while, I'm guessing."

"He'd better. Is Henry left or right-handed?"

"Right, I think."

"Well there's some good news."

Dad chuckled through his nose, looked at the floor for a moment before turning back to me.

"Did you have a good Christmas?"

"Yeah, yeah, it was really nice."

"Santa bring ya everything you wanted?"

"Aw, come on Pops."

"Because he didn't me. I need to have a talk with he and your mother for next year: no more kitschy scotch-tape dispensers. It was cute once, now I'm running out of room on my desk."

"Well personally, I liked this year's otter dispenser far more than last year's clown dispenser. That was a thing of nightmares."

"That's true. Where does she even find these things?"

"There's this place called the Internet. You can get anything there, it's amazing."

"Oh, I've heard of that!"

"It's this magical place where things you didn't even know you wanted exist, and you can buy them as long as you have an address and a credit card."

Dad goofed up his voice a bit. "Well, ain't that just sumpthin! This ol' country bumpkin ain't never gonna have to go shoppin' with the wife again! Saints be praised!"

We laughed together for an honest moment that felt good. We both needed it. Dad's dorky side had gone into hibernation for a while. It was good to see it again, bumbling out of its cave.

"Hey," he started after the laughter subsided, "I wanted to say something to you the other night."

I immediately remembered what he was referring to. It was the night we sprung the trap. It was just he and I doing last-minute tests and checks before the others came and he'd suddenly lowered every wall he ever built between us and was about to say something big. Of *course* I immediately remembered.

I nodded. "Yeah?"

"I just want to make one thing crystal clear first, all right?"
I nodded.

"Burning down that house was wrong—"

"Ahh, Jesus, Dad, really?" The blood surged to my face and I could feel my chest bubbling with sudden rage like a pot of water going from tepid to boiling in an instant. "Are you really doing this now?"

"Let me finish—"

"How many times are you going to remind me how disappointed you are in me for that, Dad? 'Cause I just want to be prepared for the speech you'll give at my wedding or any other major life event."

"Daniel—"

"No, I think it's fucked up, man! After all this..." I gestured wildly, hoping to express what I meant— "all this crap we just went through and you're dredging that up, hoping to accomplish what—making me feel bad? Why? And on Christmas?"

I stopped there, mostly because I'd momentarily run out of steam, but partly because of the way Dad's mouth was curling into a smirk. It was like he wasn't taking me seriously and was about to burst into laughter.

"Are you ready to listen to me, Daniel?"

That house. That fucking house. I will never be rid of it. It will haunt me forever.

I'll always be Firebug.

I fixed my eyes on him and he *tsk'ed* me.

"Get that petulant look off your face," he said sourly, lightly popping me upside the head. I won't lie—it did the trick, and my fury turned to surprise. Once again, completely disarmed. I couldn't respond.

"I'm gonna start over from the top, and I hope you'll rein in that knee-jerk temper of yours this time. Okay?"

I sighed in resignation.

"Burning down that house was wrong. You know that. *I* know you know that. But I have to preface what I'm about to say with that because I don't want you thinking what you did was okay, okay?"

"Okay."

Dad continued, hesitant at first. "I've been wondering how to say this for a while, a few years now in fact, and it always sounds bad so I'm just going to say it. There's no other way.

"Thank you. For burning down that house. Thank you."

I blinked, but it was one of those quick blinks where you're trying to rewet the dryness that makes your vision blurry so you can once again see the world with clarity. If I could have done the same with my ears I would have, because I was sure I'd heard him wrong. He continued.

"I never thought I would think it, let alone say it aloud to you but… That year your mother and I were separated…was bad. To say the least. Bad for everyone. We thought we were doing what was best. But we were wrong. And we didn't know it until that farmhouse went up in flames at the hands of our eldest."

Never in a million years could I have predicted this moment.

I stayed quiet and let him continue.

"Who knows what would have happened if you hadn't done that. It…woke us up, made us realize we were behaving like children. No better than you. And that's all I've really wanted to say. That, and be kinder to your mother."

If I was a cartoon character my left eyebrow would have

lifted off my face to the tune of a violin playing one string, with my head cocked and mouth folded so far down it resembled cheese dripping off a slice of pizza. But my shock at the accusation that I was somehow *unkind* quickly smoothed out to concession as a hundred recent examples of my spiteful behavior flicked through my memory.

"There is not a human being on this earth who loves you more than that woman, and I doubt if there ever will be. So, you know, think about that every once in a while. And no, she didn't put me up to this."

He stood with a deep breath, satisfied. His brow smoothed and his lips spread into a grin. He was lighter than he'd recently been, like something had been lifted off his shoulders, and it made him the tiniest bit more inviting. I would not have minded if he'd wanted to stay and chat a little more while I strung my guitar, in fact, and was surprisingly crestfallen when he made his way to my bedroom door.

"Love you, son," he said, exiting my room. "Merry Christmas."

"Love you too," I said.

He gently pulled the door closed behind him and it shut with a barely audible *click*.

CHAPTER EIGHT

Our mousetrap had fallen silent in the days approaching New Year's Eve to the point that we almost forgot it was there. Chloe didn't. She continued to be a recluse and sequestered herself to Lilly's bedroom, refusing to pee anywhere but the front yard. Twice she dropped a deuce in the corner of the living room, but we couldn't get mad at her. It was ultimately our fault.

To celebrate the welcoming-in of the New Year, Mom bought a few bottles of sparkling cider, a bag of Tostitos and seven-layer dip, and a few gallons of our favorite ice cream. The five of us sat around the kitchen table playing Pictionary and munching on bean-and-sour cream-slathered tortilla chips. It was kids versus parents, and we were leading by a hair. The digital clock on the microwave read 11:14. During a rare moment of silence between rounds (because both Soren and Lilly had gone to the bathroom and Mom was refreshing her beverage) Dad leaned over and spoke into my ear.

"Hear that?"

I listened hard, all at once acutely aware of every sound

around me: the gurgle of the cider entering Mom's crystal glass, the soft Top '40s music playing in the background, the ga*whoosh* of a toilet flushing, the heater suddenly kicking on, and the room tone in between.

"Hear what?" I asked, not finding anything particularly worth listening to.

"It worked."

And then I understood. Up until now, most nights were, at some point, chillingly disturbed by the dismal sounds of our captured mouse. Wails. Cries. Requiems. But as of tonight, they had all but vanished, and it wasn't until now that I recognized it.

I suppose I should have smiled big and toothy, or nodded in some slyly triumphant way, or given some indication that the notion we'd starved it to death was a sure sign of victory, but instead my heart dipped, and my facial expression was my heart's shadow.

"We'll give it a few more days," Dad said, "just to make sure. Then we'll open it up."

"Yeah. Okay."

At 11:55 we took some metal pots and pans from the kitchen out to the driveway. Mom did the countdown while Soren and Lilly gripped the handles of the pots and pans, ready to clang them together and raise holy hell. I stood back and watched.

"Okay, here we go!" Mom shouted. "Ten...nine...eight..."

We all joined in the countdown. "Seven! Six! Five! Four..."

Lilly shook with excitement.

"Three! Two! ONE!"

And then all in unison: "Happy New Year!"

The air rang out with metallic cracks and peals as pots

collided with pans in our very small-town celebration. Lilly's joyful screams joined the cacophony and she danced around the driveway with her kitchen instruments. Everyone was smiling. Mom rushed to join Lilly and Soren, and the three howled together into the night like a wolf mother with her pups. Dad took a step back and enjoyed his family's jubilant celebration, and I swear I saw a glimpse of what he was like as a child. Perhaps he'd engaged in similar New Year's rituals with his mom and dad and brother and the scene playing out before him was a time machine that instantly put him back there.

My heart filled up to the brim and before I knew it, was overflowing. It was the first time since Mom and Dad took me out of school that I felt I was exactly where I belonged.

A few days went by and Mom and Dad returned to work, their holiday vacations over. School was back in session, so Lilly and Soren were out of the house too. It would just be Mom and me, but she had several accounts to attend to which required her personal attention and she'd be gone until around three p.m. She'd warned me there would be a list of chores to be done when I awoke, and I wanted to delay any exertion for as long as possible.

I woke up late that Monday (late being nine a.m.) and lay in bed for a while, arms wrapped tightly around a pillow, enjoying the warmth beneath the covers. I thought about rolling over and maybe checking Facebook on my phone, maybe jerking off, or maybe just snoozing for another hour or so. The thought of having to vacuum and dust and shovel more goddamn fuck-nutting shit-pissing snow exhausted me as much as it disgusted me and I only wanted to stay there, in the fetal position, cuddling my pillow in a warm womb of soft blankets and fluff. I swore right then and there I was moving to southern California once I had my shit together. I lingered for another ten minutes or so, executing none of my three time-killing options, then got my ass out of bed. An odd restlessness had energized me, and staying in my lovely snug cocoon was no longer a choice.

I padded down the hallway wearing only boxer shorts (the black ones with skulls and crossbones printed all over them) and veered into the bathroom to take my morning piss. My reflection in the mirror caught me before I lifted the toilet lid, and I recalled when I'd first been brought back home and the state my body had been in: wasted, slight, and unhealthy. Now, after only a little more than a month at home, my body was something more familiar, and it took me momentarily off guard. There was meat back on my bones. I had muscle definition. My skin looked smooth and much less the color of a cadaver's. And then that college life, that *other* life felt so far away. It seemed light years away. And I didn't miss it.

After emptying my bladder, I shuffled to the kitchen to make a fresh pot of coffee and find something to eat. With the coffee pot gurgling and hissing, I opened the pantry and reached for a box of cereal. I poured myself a bowl of Crunch Berries, a breakfast delicacy in our household, and added just enough milk to make it "a bowl of cereal" because I hate soggy Crunch Berries. We never got sweet, sweet delicious sugary cereals growing up. We always got Grape Nuts or Bran Flakes or some form of granola bullshit, because Mom refused to buy what she called "boxes of sugar in fun shapes." But once a year, always during the holidays, she would indulge our childish need for sugar in fun shapes and angels would sing and the kids would rejoice and heaven and earth would be as one. It was a short-lived victory for us, but one we always looked forward to. And as I poured a minute amount of milk on my Crunch Berries to ensure they would, in fact, stay crunchy, I looked out the sliding-glass door into the backyard. It was the first time I'd noticed the snow was completely gone.

Much like glimpsing my healthy body in the mirror, seeing the yard without snow took me off guard and my spoonful of cereal paused just short of my mouth. There stood the trailer, our illustrious mousetrap, with not a single spot of white stuff around its ragged wheels when only just last night they had been nearly covered by it. It was like some amazing magic trick, or perhaps a parallel universe I'd just stepped into. The trees bent as periodic gusts of wind rattled their bony branches. I left my cereal and went outside, knowing that bundling up against the cold would be unnecessary.

The breeze blew warm, as warm as if it were a late spring morning. Standing there in nothing but my boxer shorts, the wind caressing my bare chest and whispering through what few hairs lived there, I stared at the trailer as intuition bloomed inside my belly. Mom and Dad would strongly disapprove of what I was about to do so I knew I had to act fast. I whirled around and went back inside to get dressed and grab the key to the locked trailer.

The Chinook had uncovered soggy brown grass that squished and squirted beneath my Vans. My long black thermal shirt pressed tightly against my body with every blast of wind and my hair blew wildly in every direction. I pressed the key tightly between thumb and forefinger in tiny pulses that matched my footsteps. I'd known where Dad stored it— in his middle desk drawer beneath a stack of manila envelopes pregnant with old paperwork—and I'd carefully removed it, noting its exact placement so I could return it and no one would be the wiser.

The trailer matched the flat gray sky in color and as I neared it, for a second or two, the sun cut through the clouds and gleamed off the silver roof. Never in all my life had I ever taken anything as a sign—it's just not how my brain was wired, how I was raised, or what my belief systems were—but given the past month of events, I took that second or two of glorious sunshine glinting off the metallic roof as a sign. Or maybe I just saw what I wanted to see. But who cares? Whether it was a cosmic go-ahead or a deadly warning to desist or simply just a natural break in the clouds, I'd made up my mind. I was opening this trailer and seeing what was inside.

I slid the key into the shielded padlock with trembling hands, half expecting an angry shout of reproach from Dad from the sliding-glass door; he'd come home unexpectedly and caught me doing something wrong yet again. But I was alone and trusted that I would be for several more hours.

With a twist the U-shaped finger popped free and I carefully removed the padlock from the latch. I lifted the metal arm that kept the door closed and stood there for a few seconds before opening it, staring dumbly at the door handle.

This could go one of two ways:

Either the *it* had been putting on a good show and knew to keep still and quiet, knew we'd open the door eventually, thereby aiding in its escape and potentially killing ourselves in the process, or—

We indeed had reduced it to a starving (or starved) worthless heap (or corpse) and our plan actually worked and the good guys had won and the thing was dead.

I watched my trembling hand grip the door handle.

The wind blasted my face and thundered past my ears. I breathed it in.

"Daniel, you're crazy," I whispered.

With an agonizing screech, the doors opened on rusty hinges and the trailer interior lay before me.

There was the tipped barbecue grill, pieces of wood charred black scattered about the trailer floor, and there was the rope, looped and limp like a thick bootlace.

But no *it*.

A queer mixture of panic and disappointment bloomed in my chest and my eyes continued to hungrily scan the trailer's interior, not believing what they were seeing.

How? How did it escape?

And when?

Sticky black claw marks streaked the sides of the trailer and shallow dents pitted the metal. The wooden plank we'd used to cover the window was almost completely black. My eyes darted to every corner, desperately seeking the hole or crack that our mouse had escaped through.

But we made sure…I know we did…Dad did too…

Movement in the far-left corner caught my eye and my heart stopped. A feeling akin to seeing an ex out in public for the first time after a breakup when your heart is still broken and they've clearly moved on seized my chest and squeezed it tightly.

A small black lump, roughly the size of an avocado (and, oddly, about the same shape) was looking at me. I'd thought it was nothing more than a cold black cinder from the toppled grill; it had blended in with the others so seamlessly. It stared back at me with those alien eyes, trembling in the corner like an abused dog. A breath was caught in my lungs. Neither of us moved. We studied each other like two wild animals negotiating whether to attack or amicably move past one another; in this situation, it was clear who the winner would be. *It* had been reduced to next to nothing, presumably through starvation, and looked to not have an ounce of fight or flight left. Our plan had worked. The good guys had won.

And I could not have felt worse about it.

Very slowly, as to not frighten it further, I knelt into a crouch. It followed my action warily with its hollow eyes and pressed itself hard into the corner. I sat on my haunches just outside the trailer, watching the timid creature watching me for a full minute. I wondered what it was thinking, what was going through its head, because about a thousand things were going through mine:

Maybe where it's from, what it eats is normal—

Maybe only to us it seems atrocious—

Because it doesn't belong here—

It doesn't belong here—

Did it come here by accident?

Is it dying?

Does it have a family of its own?

I hadn't registered the object in my pocket pressing into my thigh when I'd first crouched down but noticed it now. It felt like a tube of Chapstick or a roll of pennies. I absently touched it, traced its outline.

It was a lighter. The shape was unmistakable.

Why would there be a—

And then I remembered.

I had been wearing these jeans that night at Rebecca's. Brett had handed me his lighter and I'd lit the grocery receipt to lure the *it* away from her. Purely by habit, I must have slid his lighter into my pocket without even thinking about it. I'd rumpled and thrown those jeans into my closet where I'd found them this morning and pulled them on in my haste to get outside.

That gleam of sunlight hitting the trailer roof was now indisputably a sign.

I burrowed my fingers into my pocket and slowly, as to not agitate the tiny creature in the corner, withdrew the lighter. My hand moved unhurriedly. I held the lighter up as if to show it wasn't a weapon and I meant the creature no harm. It continued to watch me with trepidation. With a flick of the flint wheel a spiky flame came to life, and I expected an immediate change in the little mouse's demeanor. Those hollow eyes still quivered, its little black body still pressed firmly into the corner. Trust, after all that we had put this creature through, might be harder to earn than just showing it some fire.

I crouched lower, got belly-down on the ramp and was eye-level with the *it*, the flame glowing between us.

A few seconds went by.

What's your endgame, Daniel? What exactly are you doing?

I couldn't answer my own questions, not just yet, but I knew I wanted the creature to come closer. It shifted a bit, seemed to cock its head to the side. It was staring at the flame now, its curiosity perhaps getting the better of it.

"Come on," I whispered, as if coaxing a stray dog to come get some food, "I won't hurt you." Neither of us moved for several more seconds. The flame flickered and danced but did not go out even with the Chinook blowing behind me.

The creature stretched out a hand and pulled itself away from the corner. My breath caught in my throat. Slowly, it made its way toward me, half-floating, half-crawling like a soldier who'd just lost his legs in battle. My heart lifted thinking it was beginning to trust me, but I couldn't help the tiny hook of fear that tugged at my chest. It drew closer and then stopped when the Chinook finally won and blew out the flame. I quickly reignited it, but the creature did not advance.

"Come on," I whispered again. "It's okay."

Feathery strands gently spun from its head and arms, and it quickly flattened itself against the cold metal floor to regain solidity before continuing toward me. It was now only a few feet away. I delicately extended my hand, held it out palm-up, and with my other hand, brought the lighter in close. The creature stopped again, studied my outstretched hand.

"I'm not gonna hurt you," I whispered, aching at the sight of its vulnerability. We'd reduced it to nearly nothing. We'd almost destroyed it, this scientific marvel, and here it was, still taking a chance just to get closer to the flame. I felt like crying.

And then its eyes looked into mine and tears fell down my cheeks. I couldn't help it. I let them flow down my face.

"I'm sorry..." My voice was broken into pieces by my grief. Our locked eyes did not stray and neither of us blinked. It dipped its head down once more to keep itself whole, and then floated above my palm before landing on it as softly as would a butterfly. I gasped in amazement. Most, if not all animals in the wild, when their lives are threatened and a good human comes along and makes the decision to help it, flee as soon as they are rescued, unaware that a natural enemy has just saved its life. But this, our mouse, our *it*, seemed to recognize my intentions. It felt soft in my hand like I was holding a young, down-feathered bird instead of the oily-slick lump it appeared to be. The flame continued to burn between us, and a tiny mouth opened up in the creature's face to form a lowercase O, and it reminded me of a child *ooooh*-ing at something brand new and pretty. I smiled.

"I know…" I said, my voice still thick in my throat.

The Chinook gusted behind us, dry tree branches clacking together, high-pitched whistles sounding from the eaves of the house. For us, the moment slowed to the point where time no longer existed, and I was reminded of the night when I truly saw this creature for the first time at the Tomlinsons'. I'd found it dancing in the fire—no, not in the fire, *with* it—and I knew then that we, me and this creature from another place, shared something profoundly simple.

As carefully as I could, I got to my feet. The creature did not move. It stayed there, nestled in my palm, either too weak to flee in distress or trusting that I meant no harm. The lighter flame could no longer be sustained in the wind, and after five or six attempts to bring it back, I gave up. Neither of us seemed to mind.

I stepped off the ramp and onto the brown grass. The creature felt the Chinook and reacted in a way that made me think the wind was a welcomed familiarity.

"It's time for you to go back home now."

Thin black tendrils lifted from its head and arms. This

time, it did not fight it. Those strange eyes looked into mine for the last time.

The Chinook gathered in strength and the rattling tree branches filled the air with a tribal beat. Inch by inch my tiny creature evaporated into the wind until my palm was empty and all that remained was a faint black mark. I watched what it had become—a thin, twisting black vapor—disperse in the atmosphere until it was gone, and I was left alone looking at the sky like a sad child watching his lost balloon.

EPILOGUE

I returned the trailer key to Dad's desk drawer and rehearsed being surprised when we'd both inevitably go to investigate the state of our mouse in a day or two: *It must have just faded away to nothing. Problem solved. Mulder and Scully could not have done a better job.*

Despite my long list of chores, I went to my bedroom and picked up my guitar. I wrote two songs that day, a feat I had never before accomplished. I wouldn't perform them for anybody until several years later.

I didn't know if setting the *it* free was the right thing to do or the wrong thing, but in the years that followed, we never saw it again. Maybe it returned to from where it came, maybe it went on to some other part of the world or blew to a different world entirely. I made a choice that day, that's all. I chose what I felt was right.

I'm a middle-aged man now. I still play music on my acoustic guitar but as my life progressed, I fell in love with writing. I published a few novels to mediocre reviews and less-than-desirable book sales, but it's what I love and I will continue to do it. I decided early on that I would tell this story once I felt far enough removed from the events to make it sincere without being sensationalized. Absolutely everything is true. I haven't changed any names yet to protect privacy, but I imagine I will once I publish this.

I don't drink anymore. I don't light fires unless they are in a fireplace or contained within stones while camping. I took up smoking cigarettes and that is my vice, which is not at all a good tradeoff, but hey, my liver is intact and nobody else's house has burnt down. I put that in the "win" column.

The Oopsie was eventually born and given an actual name, though I did float the idea of just keeping it as is, stating no one in her class would share it and she'd probably grow up to be a famous motocross rider or the lead singer in a punk band or something. I was ignored and Mom and Dad went with Della, after Dad's grandma. We were all stoked to have a new baby sister but none more so than Lilly. "Two boys, two girls. It's called balance" she'd say like she invented the word. Della grew up never knowing the danger she'd been in that Christmas while nestled in Mom's womb, so I imagine we're going to have a long conversation once she reads this novel.

I married twice, divorced twice, and thankfully only produced one offspring to get fucked up in the mess. Her name is Ruby and she is the light of my stupid little life. When she was seven, I caught her playing with matches. I gave her a proper scolding to prevent it from happening again but couldn't help that flicker of kinship. She's seventeen now, and her Grandma and Grandpa continue to spoil her rotten.

There is not a Christmas that goes by I don't think about

that wind on *that* day leading up to the events that opened my eyes and ultimately changed my life. There is more to life than what we've seen on Earth. And even more mysteries. Whenever a Chinook blows through town, I can't help but wonder what's riding on its back.

And that's it. The end. I'm craving an American Spirit right now, and believe I've earned it. I like watching the end smolder bright red and the smoke twist lazily into the air.

THE END

ACKNOWLEDGMENTS

First, I'd like to thank every English and Literature teacher I've ever had—most notably Mrs. Vopat, Mrs. Nelson, and Mrs. Cunningham, all of them my elementary ed schoolteachers. They recognized very early on that I much preferred (and was far better at) telling stories than playing sports. Double goes for my parents, Steven Blair and Linda Earnest. The early encouragement I received from them shaped my desire to continue writing. *Firebug* would not exist without them. Nor would it exist without my initial inspiration, my dog Liesl. Playing backyard frisbee with her was the genesis of this story.

Adam Pitman and Adam Stilwell read early drafts and gave me a much-needed boost of confidence. Without their cheerleading I'm not sure I would have ever published this. I want to thank Becky Rygg and Sarina Hart for their enthused, insightful feedback. Mikey Winn was essential in the creation of *Firebug* and I've never had synergy with a colleague the way I've had with him. Thank you, Mikey!

I need to thank Jeff Giles for his attention and willingness to read some local barista's manuscript. Special thanks is owed to Jess Owen for acting as a human compass pointing the way.

Like the master Stephen King says, writing is lonely and it helps having someone believe in you...that someone is my partner Jake Carr. Thank you for pushing, inspiring, loving, and believing.

Made in United States
Troutdale, OR
06/18/2023

10654817R00130